Men of Death

by

Terry Balcombe

DORRANCE PUBLISHING CO., INC.
PITTSBURGH, PENNSYLVANIA 15222

All Rights Reserved
Copyright © 1998 by Terry Balcombe
No part of this book may be reproduced or transmitted
in any form or by any means, electronic or mechanical,
including photocopying, recording, or by any information
storage and retrieval system without permission in
writing from the publisher.

ISBN # 0-8059-4283-1
Printed in the United States of America

First Printing

For information or to order additional books, please write:
Dorrance Publishing Co., Inc.
643 Smithfield Street
Pittsburgh, Pennsylvania 15222
U.S.A.

For Billy

Acknowledgments

I would like to thank the following for their support before, during, and after the writing of this novel.

Thanks to Pat and Fred (my mum and dad), to Sam and Kevin (now you can read it), and to Billy for making me a very proud uncle.

Also thanks to everyone that I have worked with—Des, Nick, Peter, Tony, Nigel, Martin, Rickets, Jimbo, Julia, Elaine, Chris, Tami, Lis, Sat, Wendy, Sue, Natalie, Margaret, Trudy, Chum, David. Peter, and April. I know there are many more but I can't name you all, so to those I haven't named, thank you.

I would like to say a special thanks to the musicians and singers that have helped me concentrate while I played on my own keyboard (the computer variety).

Thanks to Guns 'n' Roses, The Rolling Stones, The Who, Lenny Kravitz, and Jimi Hendrix (you'll live forever). Also to David Bowie, REM, Seal, and Bob Dylan, many thanks.

Finally a thank you to the rest of my family (you know who you are). Many thanks to everyone, you'll never know just how grateful I am.

Prologue

> There must be some kind of way out of
> here, said the joker to the thief.
> — Jimi Hendrix

The two men sat patiently, waiting at the window, their target not yet in sight. Both men excelled at their job, but both men were so different. One had a heart, the other didn't.

"Where the fuck are they?" asked the younger, who was Chinese.

"Just be patient, they'll be here," said his partner.

"Well I'm getting cold and pissed off," moaned the Chinese man. The room was cold and damp, but it was an excellent viewing point. From there they could see up and down the whole street.

"You're not going to last long without patience Chang, so try keeping your mouth shut, will you?" growled Dempsey. His remark was met by a stare from Chang, a stare that showed lack of respect.

This was only Chang's second assignment, but Dempsey had half a dozen under his belt already. His experience meant he was in charge. They continued to look through the broken window, waiting for their target. Ten minutes of silence passed.

Coming down the street was a Range Rover. Chang sat up when he saw the car approaching, his sweaty hands grasping the small box that would cause the explosion.

"Steady, Chang. Remember the bomb is in the waste bin, wait until the car parks," instructed Dempsey. Whether Chang heard or not, Dempsey wasn't sure.

The car got nearer and nearer, and the closer it got, the more agitated Chang became. Dempsey suddenly saw something that he didn't like.

"There are children in the back, what are they doing there? He was supposed to be on his own. The job's off," said Dempsey. Chang still sat there, the small box in his right hand, his thumb hovering over the green button. He hadn't moved.

"I said the job's off, Chang, so drop the detonator."

The silver Range Rover came to a halt just behind the waste bin.

"I said drop it, Chang, this job is canceled."

Chang looked at his co-bomber and smiled. His thumb pressed down on the green button. Dempsey leaned forward yelling, but it was too late.

The waste bin exploded with enough force to shatter glass three hundred yards away. The blast catapulted the Range Rover into the air, engulfed by flames. As the four-wheel drive car landed on its side, it was obvious that there could be no survivors.

The window through which Chang and Dempsey were viewing was shattered by the explosion sending glass all over the damp and dingy room. Dempsey rolled off Chang and pulled the Chinaman to his feet, his fists gripping the front of the brown leather jacket that Chang wore.

Dempsey swung a hard punch into the Chinaman's midriff, doubling him over. Dempsey left him to fall to the ground.

"You mad fucker!" cried Dempsey. As he walked out, Chang began to laugh hysterically.

Chapter One

> Hey Joe, where you going with that gun in your hand
> — Jimi Hendrix

The room was poor but would be ideal for the occasion. He would need a place to retreat to after the job was done, and this room would be the last place anyone would look. After opening the windows, he turned and caught a glimpse of his reflection in the glass of an awful picture on the wall. What John Dempsey saw he hated, what he did he hated, but what he did was what he was good at.

Since leaving the SAS six years ago, he had become a professional assassin working for the British government. His targets ranged from executive businessmen who were getting too big for their boots to just about anybody who pissed off the men at Whitehall.

The years in the army had taken a toll; his body was riddled with scars and abrasions. Dempsey had barely survived a sniper attack in Northern Ireland when he was injured by a car bomb just outside of this hotel while on holiday in Israel. After recovering, he applied for the SAS and passed with flying colours. With SAS he worked undercover in the Falklands, Argentina, Libya, Israel, and Iraq. In each place he could remember someone who had asked the wrong question or had seen the wrong thing, people who had to be eliminated or risk exposing his cover. How many had he killed? Well, he knew because he could always remember the last look on each person's face; each last look was etched horribly in his mind.

The sound of his mobile phone chattering away like a canary on LSD brought Dempsey back to his senses. The phone was on the bed next to his sports holdall, and as soon as he pressed the receive button, he heard the gruff voice for which he had been waiting.

"Dempsey," answered the former military man.

"Are you where you are supposed to be?" asked the gruff voice.

"Of course I am. Which one's the target?"

"I take it you have the photograph in front of you, John," said the gruff voice. Dempsey had always been a very patient man, but it was beginning to wear a little thin by now.

"Who the fuck is the target, Chalmers?" snapped Dempsey.

"Not had a good day, John? You sound a little stressed to me. The target is our friend in the middle with the red tie. You have his name and details. Any problem with that, John?" asked Chalmers.

"What about payment?" inquired Dempsey.

"The usual way. Half is already in your account, the rest on completion of the job," said Chalmers.

"Okay, Chalmers, I'll be in touch," said Dempsey warily. He had never trusted Chalmers in the four years he had worked for him, especially after Chalmers had blackmailed him to take out a man whom Dempsey had respected and worked under in the army. They had threatened Dempsey's daughter, so he did the job—only to see his family die, anyway. Since that day Dempsey had vowed never to trust his employer for as long as he lived.

As Chalmers hung up the receiver, he heard two knocks on his office door.

"Come in Allison." It seemed almost as though he knew she was going to knock at that precise second.

"The file you asked for, sir," said Allison, as she offered the file to her employer.

"Thank you," replied Chalmers. As the secretary turned away, Chalmers' attention was attracted by the shapely behind that was leaving his office.

Chalmers wondered if he would ever have a chance with such a good looking woman. Him fifty-four, her half his age at twenty-seven. He was plump and balding. Chalmers decided that he had no chance and quickly removed the thought from his mind.

Chalmers then opened the file that Alison had just handed to him: "Stephen Edward Andrew Murray, otherwise known as John Dempsey. Joined the army, the fifteenth of July 1975. Served with the Parachute Regiment for eleven years before being shot whilst in Belfast. Spent five years in Special Air Service before being recruited as a Special Government Operative. Has successfully completed fifteen assignments, but is regarded as extremely dangerous, unpredictable, and a possible threat." Chalmers closed the file and picked up the telephone receiver. As he dialled he spoke his thoughts. "After this job John, we have what will be your final challenge."

Dempsey awoke to the sound of Coronation Street, which had just begun on television. If he had not known the signature tune, he probably would not have known what was playing on the small black and white set on top of a chest of drawers opposite him. All Dempsey could see were fuzzy, wavy lines.

Dempsey rose from the hard bed and switched the set off. He hadn't eaten since early that morning. He found it hard to eat when an assignment was in motion, but now his stomach yearned for food. Dempsey remembered a small public house just down from the bed and breakfast in which he was staying. A pint and a light meal would be enough.

The operative walked out to the very small en suite bathroom. It contained a toilet, a small basin, and a shower unit, each looking like it was in a race to produce penicillin. Dempsey pulled the cord to switch on the light (at least it worked), and then switched on the tap. He splashed water on his face, in a bid to wake himself a little, and caught sight of himself in the cracked mirror above the basin.

Dempsey ran his hands through his collar length black hair, returning it to some kind of normality. He stared at his reflection, the scar about his eye a memory of Belfast. The troubles in Northern Ireland were hard times for any soldier in the British Army. Dempsey had seen many crack under the pressure; some left, others committed suicide.

Dempsey patted the resident towel over his face. For a man of thirty-nine years, he was still in good shape. He was five feet ten, and he had weighted twelve stones for the last six years. His strong jaw and chiseled looks were good enough to woo any woman that he wanted, but that was hard for him since Carole and Lisa.

Dempsey turned off the tap and pulled the cord which switched off the light. On the floor beside the bed was a black sports holdall. Dempsey picked the bag up and unzipped it.

Inside was a spare shirt, trousers, and underwear. Also there was a holster with a .357 Magnum in it. Dempsey removed the heavy firearm from the holster and checked to see if it was loaded. When satisfied, he returned the four-inch barreled gun to the holster and lay it on the bed. Dempsey spotted the bottle of Jack Daniel's which also lay in the holdall. After completing an assignment, he always got pissed on Jack Daniel's—to him it just seemed the right thing to do.

And last but not least was the chosen weapon for his particular job, the Ingram M10 sub-machine gun. With a possible twelve hundred rounds per minute. This gun was more than necessary for what he needed.

Dempsey retrieved the holster and firearm from the bed, and then wrapped the holster around his shoulders so the .357 rested below his left armpit. After putting on his leather jacket, he checked to see if the gun was visible, and once satisfied, he returned the holdall to the floor and pushed it underneath the bed. He checked the room before he left, then switched off the light and locked the door after closing it behind him

As he reached the bottom of the stairs a door opened, and a small, frail woman with grey hair stood there.

"Is the room okay for you, Mr. Johnson?" asked the old lady. Dempsey looked at her—her appearance was that of the archetypal grandmother—something he had never had.

"Yes, the room's fine thank you," replied Dempsey, smiling at the old woman, who returned the compliment with a smile of her own.

"Remember I lock the front door at eleven."

"That's okay, I'll be back long before then."

The two exchanged farewells, and Dempsey left through the front door. He was not ready for the icy cold wind that bit into his cheeks the moment the door opened. The sky was clear, the stars were twinkling brightly, and a frost would have fallen by the morning. Dempsey shivered and placed his hands in his jacket pockets, his left fist grazing the heavy firearm that was positioned beneath his armpit. He felt comfort with the .357, an edge that he felt was missing with other hand held weapons. As he walked, the street lights shimmered on the damp tarmac of the road.

The King's Head did not have the appearance of a grand pub from the outside, but inside it was quite lavish and palatial. The size also surprised Dempsey, and momentarily the word *TARDIS* came into his head. He breathed in and smelled the aroma of furniture polish.

"What will it be then, sir?" asked the landlord. Dempsey could not help but notice that the plump, five-feet-two-inch man in front of him was wearing one of the worst hairpieces he had ever seen. Some were good, the join not always noticeable, but this was a ginger mop positioned badly on a head with grey hair at the sides.

"Pint of lager, mate, with a Jack Daniel's chaser," replied Dempsey. Wiggy nodded and set about his task. "Is there any food, or I am too late?"

"One moment and I'll get you a menu," answered Wiggy as he put the pint of lager on the bar. He rushed off and quickly returned with a menu. "I'll just get your Jack Daniel's," said Wiggy, handing Dempsey the menu.

On the menu, ham and eggs leapt out at Dempsey.

Not too heavy, the thought as he sipped at the lager. Wiggy returned with the Jack Daniel's, and Dempsey wondered if Wiggy was aware just how awful his hairpiece looked.

"Made up your mind yet, then, sir?" Wiggy asked cheerily.

"Ham and eggs please," said Dempsey, putting his hand in his pocket to search for some money.

"That'll be five-fifty, please," said Wiggy, his smile beaming like a cat that got the cream. "The food will be about ten minutes." The smile appeared to get wider and wider. Dempsey found the correct change and handed it to Wiggy, who went sauntering off to the cash register. Dempsey saw a table just behind him, so headed for it. The table was one of those small ones that was supposed to be for six people to sit around, when really three would have crowded it.

The weather had obviously deterred many people from coming to the pub that night. Dempsey looked around the bar area, noting that there couldn't have been more than a dozen people altogether. Dempsey noticed a newspaper on the seat beside him, so decided to have a look before his food arrived. The headlines were the usual slanderous rubbish found on the front pages of many grotty tabloids these days! I had sex with pop star, footballer beat me up in drunken rage, orgy at private school, etc., etc.

Unimpressed, Dempsey turned to the back pages, where he found a picture of a boxer holding his newly acquired belt. It made Dempsey remember the days when he had fought as an amateur. He had had the credentials to become ABA champion, but he broke his thumb when he fell off his pushbike, and he never boxed again. Dempsey's memories were interrupted by a soft female voice.

"Ham and eggs was it, sir?" asked the voice.

"Yes, thank you." Dempsey looked up from the newspaper to see a very pretty, early-twenties blonde woman holding his plate of food. She placed the plate on the table and handed Dempsey a knife and fork wrapped in a serviette.

"I haven't seen you in here before," she remarked.

"I'm here on business," said Dempsey. "Only here for a few days."

The young girl smiled at him. "Enjoy your meal, won't you," she said as she walked away. Dempsey's eyes remained on the young girl until she reached the bar area where a leather clad man was staring at him.

Probably just a biker, thought Dempsey as he cut the ham on his plate.

The biker continued to stare at the government operative, and soon Dempsey could feel the burning eyes looking at him.

"Susan," called the biker to the blonde girl, "so who's the prick with the ham and eggs, then?" he demanded. There was an edge to his voice.

"I don't know. He said he was here on business or something," she snapped back.

"Well he better watch himself, looking at my bird like that," rasped the biker. He returned to staring at Dempsey, who was sipping at his pint but aware that he was still being watched. Dempsey was becoming more and more annoyed with the biker. The last thing he wanted was to bring attention to himself by having a barroom brawl, but this man was beginning to get on his nerves.

The barmaid came over to Dempsey again. "Everything alright, is it?"

"Fine," replied Dempsey, glaring at the biker, who was now talking to a leather-clad friend. As they spoke, they both glanced at Dempsey, who by now had lost his patience.

As the pretty blonde walked away, Dempsey gave her a wink, making sure that the two bikers saw him do it. He wanted to do something about these two now, and the little wink was enough to start something off.

The two bikers approached him menacingly.

The boyfriend was taller than Dempsey had first thought, about six feet and quite athletic looking. His friend was smaller and a little rotund; his leathers looked too small for him.

"You got some kind of problem, mate?" said the first biker, his tone nasty.

"None that I know of," replied Dempsey calmly. He swigged the Jack Daniels.

"Well, I think you have, because you're looking at my bird a bit too much," said the biker through clinched teeth. Dempsey noticed the biker's teeth were yellow, probably the result of years of smoking.

"Come on Jimmy, let's do him," said the rotund biker. He sounded like a little kid in a playground where a bully was about to have a fight.

"In here or outside, it's your choice, you fucker," stated the boyfriend.

In the background Wiggy could be heard, telling them to leave it out and drink their drinks; the pretty blonde was doing likewise. Dempsey saw this as his moment to move. He swiftly pushed the small table in front of him into the boyfriend's legs, just above the knees. The impact caused the biker to drop forward, and in anticipation of this, Dempsey grabbed the back of his head and thrust it into the table. The crack of bone was audible when the biker's nose broke.

The plump biker watched his friend fall backwards, his hands clasped to his face. Blood cascaded through his fingers like a waterfall. The plump biker threw a straight right at Dempsey's face, but Dempsey's skill and superior agility enabled him to avoid it. He caught the biker's wrist with his right hand and then thrust his left forearm at the elbow of the rotund biker.

The result was devastating. The force of Dempsey's forearm against the joint caused the arm to go into an "L" shape against the joint. The crack of bone was heard on the other side of the pub, where people had begun to realise that some kind of fight was in progress.

The fat biker collapsed to the floor, yelping like an injured dog. Dempsey could now concentrate solely on the boyfriend, who was slowly rising to his feet. Wiggy was still yelling from the other side of the bar as Dempsey moved away from behind the small table.

Dempsey saw rage in the biker's eyes as he charged at him. Dempsey positioned himself to intercept the charging maniac who was coming towards him. At the last second Dempsey moved, flinging his arms around so they caught the biker in the back. The biker, aware of

Dempsey's sudden move, could do nothing as his momentum carried him forward. He hit the small table and sailed over it, landing in a heap, his legs in the air and his head concussed from striking the floor.

The former soldier now moved on his intended victim, pulling him off the floor by the collar of his leather jacket and swinging a punch to the biker's stomach. On impact the biker doubled over in pain, his hands not knowing whether to hold his face or his stomach.

Dempsey was still not finished. With his left hand he clinched the top of the victim's head and with the right hand drove a punch firmly into his face. The biker's bottom lip exploded with the sticky red liquid that was already streaming from his nose, and he fell to the floor, not moving. The whole fracas lasted no more than twenty seconds.

Dempsey surveyed his work and the people around him. The boyfriend was lying unconscious on the floor, blood streaming from his nose and mouth. His friend was close to passing out, his arm grotesquely bent. Wiggy stood there open-mouthed, as people began to encroach on the two bikers.

"I don't think there's any damage, only to them," remarked Dempsey, looking at the two forlorn men on the floor.

"I think you better leave," stated Wiggy. His Cheshire cat grin had disappeared and turned into a worried, apprehensive look.

Wiggy was right. If the police got called now, it could turn into a real problem. Dempsey continued to look around as he headed for the door, passing the bikers as they lay on the floor. A woman was tending to the boyfriend, mopping his face with a handkerchief, but the fat biker was alone and still writhing in agony. Dempsey left quickly and quietly.

Nine o'clock was not an unusual time for the prime minister to be involved in a meeting; in fact, if he was not involved with official engagements, a meeting was quite a usual occurrence.

But this was no ordinary meeting. What was being discussed would not go beyond the walls of Ten Downing Street. As the prime minister spoke, Leonard Chalmers and the home secretary listened in what was a very calm and pleasant atmosphere.

"Are you sure that he is right for this job?" questioned Peter Campbell, the home secretary. Chalmers' reply was confident and well-rehearsed. "There is no doubt in my mind that he is ideal for the job."

"We cannot afford to drop a bollock on this, Leonard," stated the prime minister as he sipped at a large, expensive cognac. "If there is any doubt at all, we cannot use him."

"I am confident that he won't let us down. I'm sure of it," insisted Chalmers, who was feeling a little undermined. The home secretary stood up from the comfortable settee.

"This will have to be his final assignment, if you understand my meaning, Leonard," stated Campbell as he poured himself a cognac. Chalmers nodded, understanding exactly what he meant.

The prime minister walked over to Chalmers and offered him a handshake. "We'll leave it in your capable hands then, Leonard, good evening to you."

Chalmers returned the handshake and walked to the door. Outside a man stood there, waiting to show Chalmers the way. As the door of Number Ten opened, Chalmers felt the cold icy breeze hit his face. He was pleased with what he had achieved and with what he had been entrusted to do. As he walked down Downing Street, he smiled.

Chapter Two

Dempsey awoke early; in fact, he always had since Carole and Lisa had passed away. He washed as well as could be expected in the dreary basin of the so-called bathroom. By the time he had shaved and done the necessary on the toilet, it was approaching eight o'clock. There was a news agent quite close so he decided to buy a newspaper. Remembering the rubbish he was reading last night, he decided to buy a proper newspaper.

The pub last night, what was he thinking of, he thought. Beating two men senseless and enjoying it as well. What he had done last night was what he was good at. Violence was all he knew.

He put on a shirt and his jacket, leaving his holstered .357 in the holdall. He positioned it under the bed, out of arm's reach. Who knows who might come to the door? It wouldn't look good if he opened the door and there lying on his bed was a handgun. As he smiled there was a knock at the door. Dempsey looked at the bag down by the bed and wondered whether he should arm himself or not. He decided not to.

As he opened the door the figure in front of him caused him to swallow hard.

"Good morning sir. My name's PC Lambert," said the young man in front of him.

Come on Dempsey, don't panic.

"I understand you were involved in a disturbance last night, sir," said the officer.

"Er yes, that's right, officer," replied Dempsey.

He might have to die if he does not go.

"We were called by the hospital when they were admitted. Our investigation led us here."

Please go away or you will die.

"They've decided not to press charges, but I thought I would come here and have a chat, anyway," commented the young officer. "May I come in for a moment?"

Dempsey could hardly refuse, so he ushered in the policeman. Dempsey was surprised at how young the policeman was. Probably early twenties, he thought.

"Didn't catch your name sir."

"Bob Johnson," replied Dempsey.

"I understand you're here on business, is that right?"

Dempsey replied with a nod of his head.

"What kind of business is that, then, sir?"

"I sell stationery to large firms, paper, pens, paper clips that sort of thing. I was hoping to finalise the deal today or tomorrow," said Dempsey, continuing the lie with a very straight face.

"Well I suggest you finish your business as quickly as possible. Those two yobs might want to get their own back on you," commented the policeman sympathetically.

"Yes, I will as soon as possible."

"One more thing, sir," added the officer. "Next time you decide to take on the scum of the earth, be careful because they might hit back."

Dempsey nodded again, unsure of what he meant. He supposed the young man thought he was giving good advice, advice to a trained killer.

"Good day to you then, sir," Dempsey said as he opened the hotel room door. He closed the door behind him and began to wonder.

Would the officer check out the name he gave him?

Would he return?

Would he be alone?

After questioning himself, Dempsey decided the job would need to be done today. Then get the hell out, and wait for the next job. He bent down and picked up the holdall. After placing it on the bed he opened it and took out the envelope containing the photograph. Also inside was a list of places the target frequented. Dempsey was lucky because today was the target's day off. A day he played golf and mixed with friends at the local private club. Today, though, would be his last round of golf.

Dempsey remembered an ordinance survey map in the bedside cabinet; he got it and unraveled it. He found the course instantly and began to plan the hit.

He decided to wait for the target after he had played his round of golf, hitting him probably on the road. In this area of Kent, the roads leading to golf courses were usually quite built-up with trees and hedges. Dempsey fished in the holdall once again, pulling out the Ingram. He slammed in the magazine, then rested the sub-machine gun in his hand. It wasn't heavy and wasn't too big, either. He guessed the journey to the golf course would take approximately twenty minutes. His target teed off at ten o'clock every Thursday without fail. He had plenty of time to prepare himself for what he does best.

He decided now would be a good time to leave, just in case the young PC decided to make a return visit. He assured himself that everything was in the holdall that might incriminate him if he left it behind—the jeans, a shirt, a sweater, a pair of underpants, and the bottle of Jack Daniel's. He returned the envelope and the Ingram sub-machine gun to the bag and zipped it up. He checked his .357 and returned it to its holster. He also took the mobile phone out of his inside jacket pocket and switched it off. The last thing he wanted was to be disturbed; concentration was of the essence. Dempsey opened the door of the hotel room and locked it behind him. In six or seven hours, the job would be done, he thought. Then he left.

Chapter Three

The bulldog and the Staffordshire bull terrier were busy devouring several tins of food when Charles Lomax walked in to his kitchen.

"Those bloody dogs eat too much," he rasped at his wife. "I don't suppose there's any tea left in the pot, is there?"

"Yes, I've just made it," replied June Lomax.

They had been married for thirty-two years now, mainly happy but with its ups and downs. Five years ago she had threatened to leave him after finding out about an affair he was having with a younger woman. Lomax decided a divorce would not only be very damaging but very expensive, so he got rid of the mistress, and, with the promise of many expensive gifts, he pleaded for forgiveness. And of course he got it.

As he poured his cup of tea he looked at his watch. No rush, he thought. Still plenty of time.

"What are you up to today then, dear?" he asked his wife.

"Not much, just some shopping then lunch with Barbara," she replied.

"I haven't made all this money for you to spend on a new dress every week for Christ's sake," he bellowed. "One day it'll all run out, then what will you do, ay?"

June Lomax had heard all this before and decided she did not want to hear it again today. She stopped reading the woman's magazine and rose from the breakfast bar.

"See you later, dear," she commented as she got up, and walked out of the kitchen. Her husband continued to bellow at her until he heard the front door slam, and continued to mutter to himself about how useless women were and what their role in society should be.

After finishing his tea, Lomax decided to head for the golf course. He felt good and started to dream of a seventy-six or seventy-seven, which two or three years ago he was quite capable of attaining. He had once gotten down to almost scratch but then business intervened for a few months and his game went to pieces for a while.

After placing his golf clubs in the boot, Lomax checked he had everything he needed, and satisfied himself that he had. He would be meeting his old business partner, Brian Williams, as he had every Thursday for the last two years. He opened the door of the Mercedes Benz and climbed inside, slamming the door behind him. As he fiddled with the radio, he caught a glimpse of the house he had owned for the last ten years. If he had not knuckled down when he was younger the house in front of him would have been just a dream. Success could only yield a house like this.

Indeed, he was a success story. He had founded his own print business when he was just twenty-one and built an impressive empire. Fifteen years ago he was offered six million pounds for the business by a large company. He accepted the deal and decided to use some of it to buy property. Everything Lomax touched turned to gold; in fact, a newspaper article had dubbed him the King Midas of industry. The most work he did now was signing letters and cheques.

He was very politically minded as well and had often thought of standing for Parliament. At the moment, though, he backed the local Labour politician all the way. Next week he would be meeting the Labour party leader to discuss a donation of money and how he could help oust the present Government. Charles Lomax carried a lot of clout in business circles, and if he could persuade certain companies that Labour was the way to go, then he would. He grinned, feeling pleased with what he had done with his life. As he began to drive away he continued to try and get himself up by thinking about a seventy-five or a seventy-six.

As Dempsey drove down the country roads, he saw the sign he was looking for—Woodlands Private Golf and Country Club, one mile down on the left. Dempsey suddenly felt a strange tingle, a feeling he often got before a hit. As he approached the club, he surveyed the road, looking for a suitable place to do the kill. The golf club appeared from nowhere on the left. Just past the entrance, about fifty yards down, Dempsey spotted a small grass verge. By parking there, he would have a perfect viewing point but would be quite noticeable to traffic. The car was a hire car anyway, and it wouldn't matter because he gave a false name.

He parked on the verge, then got out and raised the bonnet. Not the best cover in the world but it had worked on a previous assignment. If anyone came and asked, he was simply waiting for a breakdown vehicle. Perfect, he thought.

Fifteen minutes and twelve expensive-looking cars later, Dempsey spotted the silver-grey Mercedes. The number plate read LOMAX1. Dempsey sneered as he saw it, thinking what a fat, rich bastard Lomax was. The Mercedes roared into the small car park and came to a sudden halt, causing a small cloud of dust. Lomax clambered out of the German car and walked around to the boot. After removing his golf clubs, he locked the boot and the car door. Wearing a red sweater and light blue slacks, he looked every part the golfer. Dempsey looked at his watch and guessed he would be waiting for another five hours or so. He had bought some sandwiches on the way, as well as two cans of lemonade and a newspaper. The newspaper would bide the time, and the sandwiches and drink would stop his stomach from growling. He lay in wait.

Leonard Chalmers had gotten to his office early that morning, knowing he had to finalise a very important job. He would wait for Dempsey to phone to say the job was done, which was usual procedure, then he would offer the next job to Dempsey, knowing full well he would accept. How did he know Dempsey will accept such a difficult assignment? Chalmers will offer top money for it, that's why. For the Lomax contract, Dempsey was getting seventy-five thousand pounds; for the next assignment, Chalmers will offer half a million. Dempsey would agree without even thinking about it.

Chalmers had eight operatives working under him, each one trained to kill with his bare hands. Each one from a different background, and each one with a different character. But they all had one thing in common: They were all experts at killing.

Due to the seriousness of this upcoming hit, Dempsey would also have to be terminated. Chalmers knew the very man and decided to give him a call. The telephone rang for a few seconds, then there was a reply.

"Yeah, who is it?"

"Robert, it's Leonard Chalmers."

"What can I do for you, Leonard? I hope it's work," answered Robert Chang with a slight accent.

"I have a job for you, Robert. Can we meet?"

"No problem, how about Luigi's wine bar, about twelve?" replied Chang.

"See you there," remarked Chalmers, and hung up the telephone receiver.

"Good shot, Charlie," remarked Lomax's golf partner, Brian Williams.

"Thanks Brian, a par here for a round of seventy-four, I do believe," replied Lomax, gloating uncontrollably.

"You've certainly left me for dead today, Charlie," said Williams as he began to pull his trolley behind him. Lomax placed his golf club back in its bag and scurried after his partner.

"So Brian, have you thought anymore about my proposal?" questioned Lomax.

"About donations for the Labour party, you mean." Lomax nodded, and his colleague continued, "Give me more information, Charlie, and I'll definitely consider it."

Williams came across his ball and surveyed his next shot.

"What do you reckon, Charlie, four iron?" queried Williams as he grasped the club. Lomax nodded in agreement and folded his arms in anticipation of the shot. Lomax had always thought his playing partner had an ungainly swing, but when Williams connected with the ball, it certainly went where it was intended to go, as it did this time. The ball bounced just before the green but continued to make its way towards the flag.

"Great shot, Brian," congratulated Lomax as the ball came to a halt about five feet from the flag.

"Too late for heroics now, Charlie, isn't it?" Williams replied, gleaming after his last shot.

Leonard Chalmers walked into the wine bar at about one o'clock. He spotted Robert Chang at a table.

"Sorry I'm late, Robert. Held up at the office," said an apologetic Leonard Chalmers.

"No worries. How are you?"

"Fine, thanks. How was Hong Kong?"

"No problems at all, now what is it I can do for you?" asked Chang as he motioned to a fellow behind the bar. Chalmers and Chang had always had a good working relationship. For some reason Chalmers treated him differently than all of his other operatives.

"Business, Robert, important business," stressed Chalmers. The chap behind the bar approached with a glass and opened a bottle of wine, placing both on the table.

"Sauvignon Blanc from Australia. I'm sure you'll like it," said Chang.

"I heard you bought in to this place, Robert," stated Chalmers as Chang poured the wine.

"Luigi needed some cash, seems like a good investment at the moment." Chang's eyes wandered around the spacious winebar in an appreciative way. "So what do you have for me? It must be important to get a personal visit." Chang swallowed some of the wine, and a cigarette burned away in his other hand.

"This is a need-to-know-only situation. Within the next two weeks a member of the government will be hit by a government operative."

As Chang nodded, Chalmers gulped some of the wine and raised his eyebrows in appreciation. "The operative cannot be allowed to live, for obvious reasons, you understand. I want you to eliminate that operative so there will be no possible comeback," finished Chalmers with another gulp of the wine.

"Who is the operative, Leonard?" demanded Chang.
"Someone you know well," replied Chalmers. "John Dempsey."
A smile appeared on Chang's face.

"I thought you would like it, Robert. One hundred and fifty thousand pounds, half now, the other half after the job is done," explained Chalmers.
"I owe that fucker," rasped Chang, remembering what had happened three years ago. "Does he know I lived after he shot me?"
Chalmers shrugged his shoulders, not knowing the answer. Chang smiled and raised his glass to his employer.
"Cheers," he said thankfully.

Lomax was over the moon with his round of golf and could not stop telling everyone. He did, indeed, par the final hole and finished with a round of seventy-four, his best for over a year. He had celebrated with a pint of bitter in the club bar.
"Same time next week, then Brian," gloated Lomax.
"Give us a chance next time, Charlie, will yer?" replied Brian Williams, who was fed up with Lomax's boasting but was also pleased for him.
Lomax left the bar area of the club and headed for his car. As he walked, there seemed to be a bounce in his step, to match the broad grin across his face. Lomax unlocked the Mercedes and jumped inside (he had put his clubs in the boot earlier). After shutting the door, he pressed a button to turn on the radio, and Led Zeppelin blared out "Stairway to Heaven." Lomax decided to turn the sound down and then proceeded to pull away.
Dempsey was ready and waiting. As soon as he saw Lomax on the move, he rushed out and closed the bonnet, started his engine, and prepared to follow. Lomax exited the car park and turned right; Dempsey followed. The plan was to ram the back of the Mercedes, which would certainly cause Lomax to stop. Dempsey would plead for mercy, and when the moment was right, *Bang, you're dead.*
The hire car sped up to the Mercedes, and just as Lomax slowed down there was contact. Both cars came to a halt, and both men jumped out.
"Sorry, mate. I wasn't looking," said Dempsey innocently. Lomax inspected the back of his car and found a broken light.
"Wasn't looking, what were you doing, you bloody fool?" bawled Lomax.
"Look, I said I was sorry, didn't I?" continued Dempsey with the act.
Lomax looked at him and smiled. "You've caught me in a good mood, my friend. We'll do the necessary exchange of addresses and insurance companies and forget about it, okay?"
Dempsey nodded and returned to his car. He reached over to the holdall and removed the Ingram from the bag. Dempsey quietly attached

a silencer and took a deep breath. The sub-machine gun was ready to do the business and so was Dempsey. As usual right before a hit, Dempsey began to sweat. He walked over to the driver's side of the Mercedes.

"Here you are," commented Dempsey.

Lomax looked up, his face suddenly grimaced in terror as Dempsey fingered the trigger. In three seconds, six shots were fired. The first hit Lomax squarely in the forehead, causing an explosion of red, pink, and grey globules out the back of his head. The second hit him in the eye, which popped like a bubble, and the third hit him in the mouth, shattering his teeth and jaw like glass. Blood sprayed the inside of the car. As Lomax fell back, Dempsey pumped three more shots into his chest. When Lomax stopped moving, Dempsey surveyed his work. The windscreen was caked with the inside of Lomax's head. Dempsey noticed a small piece of grey matter fall from the windscreen. The interior of the car was a red and grey mess.

Dempsey turned and headed for his hire car. A cold wind blew, giving an eerie sound as it passed through the trees. Dempsey did not run but walked very determinedly, looking cautiously behind him and ahead of him. There was no one around.

As Dempsey drove away, his eyes were fixed to the rearview mirror, waiting for something or someone. To ease the tension he turned on the car radio, he laughed when he heard the end of "Stairway to Heaven."

Chapter Four

Leonard Chalmers had just parked his Jaguar XJS and was about to get out when he heard his mobile phone singing away in his jacket pocket. He took it out and pulled the aerial of the telephone, then pressed the "receive call" button.

"Hello, Leonard Chalmers speaking," he uttered.

"This is Dempsey. The job's completed."

"Good," replied Chalmers. "Where are you?"

"I'm at Dartford train station in Kent."

"We have to meet today, John. I have an important job waiting for you."

"Can't it wait until tomorrow?"

"I'm afraid it can't. I have to see you today," insisted Chalmers. "Look, let's discuss it somewhere private, a winebar or a restaurant maybe."

There was a short pause. "Okay. How about the Red Lion on Mermaid Street, around eight?"

"That place is a shithole, John! There must be somewhere else," blurted Chalmers, but Dempsey had already hung up. Chalmers returned his mobile to his jacket pocket. As he opened his car door he muttered just one word. "Bastard."

A passing motorist found the dead body of Charles Lomax at around four o'clock, and the police had responded quite quickly (almost as quickly as the press, who once again were there before anyone). But by five o'clock that evening it was already beginning to get dark which was not helping the police in their duties.

The area had already been cordoned off when the blue Sierra pulled up. Two men jumped out, one wearing a black leather jacket and the other wearing a brown one. As they approached, both men showed warrant cards. A young policeman ushered them toward the Mercedes, where a woman stood.

"What we got then, Maggie?" asked Detective Inspector Peter Grant. He noticed how pale she looked as she answered.

"A right bloody mess, sir."

Grant noticed a kind of quivering in her voice. As he looked towards the car, three men were fixing a screen up around it so onlookers (mainly the press) couldn't have a good look at the crime scene.

Grant walked over to the car, closely followed by his sergeant and the female detective constable. As he poked his head into the car, the smell of death hit him. The body of Charles Lomax was just about on the turn. Lomax's trousers were stained not only with blood but with excrement from when his bowels had finally collapsed. Grant had smelled it before on a previous case involving a serial killer. He had solved that case under increasing pressure and was tipped for promotion because of it.

At just thirty-eight years of age, Detective Inspector Peter Grant was already tipped to be a superintendent before he was fifty. He communicated well with other officers, and he had respect from almost everyone in the force, something required when you move upstairs.

With freckles and red hair, Grant looked even younger than what he was. He worked out quite regularly and had even taken part in the London marathon a couple of years ago. His police work wasn't applauded by everybody, though. His wife worried about him all the time, pressuring him constantly to go for a more safer line of work, even office work. But Grant was built to catch the scum that roamed the streets. He knew that and deep down his wife knew it, too.

"Jesus Christ," muttered Grant as he saw the bloody mess in front of him. "Who was it?"

"Charles Lomax, according to his wallet," replied the detective constable. "Prominent businessman of the area."

"Are SOCO on their way?" asked Detective Sergeant Miller, who had also surveyed the interior of the car.

"Yes, they're on their way," replied WDC Maggie Thomas.

"Good," nodded Grant. "Any witnesses at all?"

"So far only the man who found the body, sir," said Thomas. "Will you want to speak to him?"

"In a moment. Well, Graham, any ideas?" Grant questioned his sergeant.

"Looks like a professional hit to me," replied Miller, who again was inspecting the inside of the car. "Whoever wanted him dead definitely made sure of it."

"Okay, Graham, take a ride up to the golf club and see what you can find out about our Mr. Lomax. By the way he's dressed, he was either leaving or going there."

Miller nodded his head and scurried off. Grant turned to the woman detective constable, who was still looking a little pale even with the two-tone flashing lights on her face.

"Okay, Maggie, where's this chap you were on about?" asked the inspector.

"This way, sir," replied Thomas.

By the time John Dempsey got home to his flat in southwest London, it was almost six-thirty. As he put the television on and poured himself a large glass of Jack Daniels, a news programme was just starting. The head story was the murder of prominent businessman Charles Lomax. As the reporter babbled on about the murder, Dempsey swallowed almost all of his drink and grimaced as the burning liquid slid down his throat.

That look on Lomax's face would be another that would be etched on Dempsey's memory. Dempsey got up and poured another large drink, and sipped at it as the report continued. On the TV was a police officer asking for help from anyone who saw anything. According to the reporter, it was a motiveless assassination.

If only it was, thought Dempsey, who by now was pouring a third Jack Daniels. Motiveless! Fucking motiveless! Every murder he had carried out was motiveless. It was time to stop. He had made his money from it and now was suffering. The next job Chalmers wanted him to do would be his last. Then no more pain, no more suffering; perhaps those memories would finally leave him. Dempsey saw a picture on the bookcase of his wife and daughter, and tears began to well up in his eyes. If it weren't for his job, they would still be alive. He slumped back onto the armchair and gulped down his drink. If only they were still alive.

Doctor Liam Kennedy had performed many post-mortems in his career, but not many like this. The bespectacled doctor had been asked to complete this postmortem as quickly as possible, and postpone other duties until it was done.

Grant and Thomas were waiting in the corridor for the results when Dr. Kennedy appeared in his blood-stained gown. His spectacles rested low on his nose.

"There are six entry wounds on his body, and two exit wounds. I've extracted all four bullets, all high impact for a single, semi-automatic weapon," stated the doctor, who with one long finger pushed his spectacles up to the bridge of his nose.

"Time of death, Liam?" asked Grant. Both men had been friends for a long time and were on first name terms.

"I would say around three, three-thirty," replied Kennedy. "They were fired from very close to cause that kind of damage, probably only a matter of feet."

"Any chance of the report by the morning, Liam?" inquired Grant.

"I'll do my best, Peter, but he's not the only stiff in here, you know. See you later." Kennedy turned and continued down the corridor as the detectives looked on.

"Right, back to the factory for a gathering. I want this sorted out as soon as possible."

Thomas nodded in agreement, and they left.

The Red Lion on Mermaid Street was as Chalmers had described it: a shithole. It was, though, one pub in which Dempsey felt at home. The opposite could be said of Chalmers. He preferred restaurants or wine bars for important meetings, not shitty little back street pubs.

As Chalmers entered, he immediately felt the stares from the regulars. Everyone wore jeans and sweatshirts and various T-shirts. Chalmers had on one of his finest Saville Row suits and camel-backed coat. If anyone looked out of place, he certainly did.

After inspecting the inside of the pub, trying to look through the fog of cigarette smoke, Chalmers spotted Dempsey and began to walk over to him.

"Nice place, John, nice class of people," remarked Chalmers, glancing around. "Are the glasses clean or do they come with free salmonella?"

Dempsey gave a hint of a chuckle and thought, *what a wanker Chalmers is. A snotty, upper-class, rich wanker.*

"This one's on me, Chalmers." Dempsey signaled to the young barmaid behind the bar, and she started pulling a pint of bitter. "So what's so important that it drags you out of your plush office?"

"I'm not sure we can talk here. There's too many ears around."

Dempsey turned on him. "Bollocks! Here or nowhere."

When the pint of bitter appeared in front of Chalmers he looked at it as if it were some kind of poison.

"It won't kill yer, take my word for it," commented Dempsey.

"I have a very important job for you, John." Chalmers put his hand in his inside pocket and drew out a folded envelope. "The necessary information is inside."

"I haven't said I'll do it yet."

"Half a million, John, that's how important this is."

"Five hundred thousand for a hit? Who the fuck is it, the Queen?"

"James Webster," replied Chalmers. "Heard of him?"

"The foreign secretary. He must of pissed somebody off," remarked Dempsey.

Chalmers looked at Dempsey until he had the hitman's full attention.

"He hasn't yet but he will, at a conference in two weeks time. His speech will malign the future of the prime minister."

"Why not just sack him instead of blowing him away?" responded Dempsey as he sipped at his lager.

"Not that easy, I'm afraid. He'll tell all anyway. He has ambition and if this brought down the PM, he'd run as a candidate and probably win." Chalmers picked up the pint of bitter and noticed a smear of lipstick on the side, so he returned it to the table. "So, John, do we have a deal?"

"Half a million, yeah?" queried Dempsey.

Chalmers nodded at him. "The usual way John—half before, half after. Well, do we have a deal or not?"

Dempsey took the envelope and put it in his pocket. Chalmers got up to leave when Dempsey spoke. "One more thing Chalmers. This is the last one. No more after this. I'm finished."

Chalmers looked at him and nodded. This will definitely be your last one, Dempsey, he thought.

Chalmers turned and immediately walked into a drinker, spilling the man's beer.

"Watch it, you prick," roared the drinker. Chalmers held his hands up in apology and hurried out through the double doors. Dempsey looked on, still slightly dumbstruck about the job. Half a million would be enough to fuck off to anywhere. He picked up his glass and finished his lager, then headed for the exit.

The disgruntled drinker was still moaning about his spilled lager when Dempsey passed him.

"Your mate's a bit of a wanker, ain't he?"

Dempsey looked on, wondering if the drinker was talking to him or not.

"You talking to me, mate?" asked Dempsey.

"Are you fucking stupid or what?" said the drinker, spittle spraying out of his mouth and covering Dempsey's face.

The drinker didn't know it was coming until it hit him. With all his force, Dempsey brought a right-handed punch through to his opponent's stomach. The drinker gasped for breath as Dempsey began to pass.

"You're right, though. He is a wanker," said Dempsey to his fallen opponent. With that, he left.

Robert Chang and John Dempsey had only one common link: They were both good at eliminating people. Dempsey was a very deeply troubled man, very much within himself. Chang was an extrovert who loved the feel of death. He thrived on it, having no scruples, no feelings, no political views, and no problem with killing absolutely anyone. As long as he got paid, he didn't care.

Although Chang worked mainly for Chalmers, he had sold his skills to other organizations. These included the Triads, who had used him on at least three occasions. In fact, his reputation had preceded him. But Robert

Chang had problems: He used cocaine regularly and often woke up not knowing where he was.

Chang was especially looking forward to his next assignment. He had vowed revenge three years ago after surviving a near fatal shot fired by Dempsey. Chang had killed Dempsey's wife and daughter after holding them hostage under orders from Chalmers. Dempsey was being blackmailed by Chalmers to do a hit, Chang got overexcited and shot them both in a moment of madness. Dempsey had fired back, and left believing that Chang was dead. If Dempsey had shot Chang in the head instead of the chest, Chang would certainly have died.

Now Chang was short of the drugs that he constantly yearned for and had arranged a meet with a pusher. The luxury flat he had in Docklands was just part of the wealth he had accumulated throughout his violent career. He had a Porsche outside, as well as an Aston Martin Volante in his garage. The share of the wine bar would also make a good profit. Paying for the drugs was never a problem for Chang, but he did not like parting with his money.

As he sat on the luxury leather settee, he pulled out a gun from the holster under his armpit. Weighing around two pounds, the 9mm Beretta fitted Chang's hand like a glove. As he slammed in the fifteen round clip, he heard the buzzer of his intercom. Chang walked over to it and picked up the receiver.

"Robert Chang speaking, who is it?"

"A friend with some merchandise."

"You best come up then." Chang pressed a button which released the entry door. Then he opened his own front door and returned to his seat, replacing the weapon back in its holster.

After a minute or so, Chang heard his front door close, and a coloured man entered, wearing a suit and carrying a briefcase.

"Pleased to meet you Mr. Chang."

Chang rose from the settee, and they shook hands. "Please, call me Robert."

"My name is Clyde Draper," replied the coloured man.

"Well then, Clyde, what do we have then?"

The pusher opened the case and put it on the coffee table in front of him. The case contained six four-inch-by-four inch sachets of white powder.

"May I?" asked Chang.

"Certainly, Robert. Go ahead," replied Draper. Chang noticed a certain hint of cockiness in the pusher's voice. Chang smiled. *Stupid fucker*, he thought. The pusher produced a knife from his pocket, and after touching a button, the blade popped out.

Draper smiled as he flipped the knife over from handle to blade, offering Chang the knife. Change accepted the knife and made a small hole in one of the sachets. Chang then sucked his index finger, put it in the sachet, then returned it to his mouth. After rubbing his finger around his gums, Chang smiled.

"How much?"

"For you, Robert, six grand per bag," responded the pusher in a tone that said I'm giving it away.

"Do you want the money now?"

"If you've got it, my man."

"Your knife, I believe," said Chang as he inspected the blade. As Draper rose from the settee opposite, Chang's arm came over like a flash. The blade spun through the air, then lodged in Draper's chest. Draper grasped at the wound, which had begun to bleed profusely. Draper slumped back into his seat, his eyes almost popping out of his head. Chang calmly walked around the coffee table.

The drug pusher was in obvious pain, but this did not deter Chang. He stood if front of Draper and clasped his hand around the handle of the weapon.

"I'm sorry, did that hurt, Clyde?" As he spoke, Chang tugged at the knife, finally freeing it from the victim's chest. Draper was on the point of unconsciousness when Chang made his next callous move.

With one swift swipe of the knife, Draper's throat was cut. The wound in his chest suddenly meant nothing as red rivulets of blood began to trickle down him. Draper's head lolled back, his body had given up on him. With the head positioned as it was, the full extent of the final injury could be seen. A vent, fully four inches horizontally across the throat, was visible.

Chang took a handkerchief from his pocket and wiped the blade, looking at his victim then at the amount of blood that had stained his white leather furniture. As he observed his handiwork he began to smile. "Didn't like the colour, anyway."

The cocaine would keep Chang going for a couple of weeks. After that, he would probably arrange to meet another drug dealer and would go through the whole process once again. The killer took another look in the case. That white powder looked so inviting to him, he had to have some. He couldn't hold on any longer.

With the knife, Chang got out a small piece of the powder and tipped it on to the table in front of him. Still using the knife, he chopped the blade over the powder in order to make it a little more fine. Chang dropped his head to the mound of cocaine in front of him and inhaled. Within seconds the small pile had gone, and Chang raised his head and wiped at his cocaine-covered nostrils. As his head went back, his eyes began to roll. Robert Chang was in ecstasy.

Chapter Five

Peter Grant was amazed at the size of the Lomax house. For a moment, his imagination ran away: There must be six or seven bedrooms, three bathrooms, swimming pool, Jacuzzi, and a snooker table, Grant mused. He wasn't far wrong, except for the snooker table. Charles Lomax had loathed snooker.

As the blue Mondeo pulled up to the front of the house, both Grant and his sergeant were weary. They had left the station at around one-thirty and were back on the job by eight in the morning. As far as evidence went, they had little to go on. Interviewing June Lomax so soon after the death of her husband might be a bad move, but no one knew how she would react.

Grant rang the front door bell, and a small woman wearing a bright pink dress answered. The colour took Miller back a little.

"Yes, what can I do for you gentlemen?" said the woman.

"Detective Inspector Peter Grant, madam, and this is Detective Sergeant Miller," replied Grant as both men showed her their warrant cards. "Could we possibly speak to Mrs. Lomax?"

"The doctor has just sedated her," said the woman. Grant looked at her as though that should not stop her speaking to him. "Very well, come in and I will find out how she's feeling." The lady in pink opened the door wider and both policemen entered.

After entering through the oak-paneled front door, Miller looked at his superior and raised his eyebrows. The inside of the house was everything Grant had imagined. Paintings on the wall, a plush staircase, and the smell of polish. There was no carpet on the floor of the entry and hall, only an extremely well-polished parquet flooring.

As they continued looking at the view, the lady in pink reappeared.

"Mrs. Lomax has agreed to talk to you, please come this way." She began to walk towards an open door, and both policemen followed. As they entered the room, a woman around fifty-five was seated on a sofa next to a young man, who was comforting her.

"Mrs. Lomax, sorry to bother you. I'm Detective Inspector Peter Grant and this is Detective Sergeant Graham Miller." Again both men showed their warrant cards. "We'd like to ask you some questions about your husband, if we may."

June Lomax responded with a nod of her head and a sniffle.

"And you are, sir?" inquired Grant to the young man.

"James Lomax. It was my father who was murdered."

Grant returned his attention again to the deceased man's wife. Miller had his notebook in his hand, like a waiter waiting for an order in a restaurant.

"Do you know of any enemies your husband might have had?" asked Grant.

"None at all," responded the widow.

"Any problems with the business?"

James Lomax fidgeted in his seat and shook his head.

"Not as far as I am aware." June Lomax looked at her son, seemingly asking for help.

"No problems at all, inspector," stated the son. "I hope you get this bastard."

"We are exploring all avenues, sir," interrupted the sergeant.

"What time did your husband leave yesterday, Mrs. Lomax?" questioned Grant.

"Well, I had already left, but he usually leaves around nine-thirty."

"Usually! This was a regular thing, then?"

"He played golf every Thursday without fail. Usually with Brian Willliams," said June Lomax.

Grant glanced at his sergeant, and Miller looked back at him, confirming he had written down the name. Grant looked back at the widow, noticing that her eyes were beginning to well up.

"Don't you think that's enough for now, inspector?" interrupted James Lomax. He gave Grant a discernful look and put his arm around his mother, who had broken down in tears.

"Okay, that's enough for now. We'll come back at a less distressing time," said Grant as he motioned to Miller. "We'll see ourselves out, madam. Good day to you."

Both men turned to leave when James Lomax spoke. "I hope you're doing more than just wandering around asking useless questions. There's a murderer out there somewhere. Find him!"

Grant understood that James Lomax was distressed, so decided not to argue. He left to the sound of June Lomax crying.

On returning to the Mondeo, Peter Grant turned to his sergeant. "Check out this Brian Williams character, see what you can dig up. Also do a check on young James Lomax."

"Do you think the son might be involved, Guv?" asked Miller.

"Someone stands to make a lot of money from Lomax's will. It might be James Lomax. He definitely seemed edgy."

"She said he played golf every week at the same time, Guv. If it was a professional hit, they would have had plenty of time to suss him out."

"We'll see what comes up then. Now how about some breakfast?" said the inspector, patting his stomach.

When John Dempsey was about to do a job he always went to see Bernard Cohen. Cohen was the owner of a small tailor's shop in the high street. It was not a suit Dempsey went there for, though; it was what Cohen had in his cellar that interested the hitman. In Bernard Cohen's cellar was a mass of guns and enough weapons to start a small war.

As soon as Dempsey entered the shop, he heard the loud greeting of the small Jewish man.

"Johnny boy, pleased to see you again," Cohen shouted.

"How are you, Bernie?" answered Dempsey.

"Was that your handiwork down in Kent the other day?"

"Yeah, it was. Can we talk business, Bernie?" asked the assassin.

"Certainly, my boy." Cohen walked to the shop door and turned the sign to "Closed" then he put a latch on the door and pulled down a blind. "Come on Johnny, you know the way."

Dempsey headed for the door in the corner, with the elderly tailor in tow. As they began to descend a flight of stairs, Dempsey retrieved a large, padded envelope from his pocket.

"The Ingram worked a treat, Bernie. Here's the rest of the money I owe."

Cohen held out his hand. "They're called Mac 10s now, Johnny, not Ingrams."

Dempsey shook his head as a schoolboy would if he had been reprimanded by his teacher. At the foot of the stairs was the doorway to another room. The small Jewish man brushed past the assassin so he could punch in the code on the security system. After pressing a series of numbers (which Dempsey knew anyway), the door clicked open.

"Come in, my boy," insisted Cohen.

Dempsey had befriended Bernard Cohen after his time in Ireland. They met up one night in a pub, both telling their relevant sob stories of years gone by. Cohen had actually listened, unlike many others who just did not have interest or compassion. Bernard Cohen had both of these in him. Dempsey had never asked how old the tailor was but guessed he was at least seventy. Cohen had told of the pain he went through in the second world war, and how lucky he and his wife were to survive. At the moment, he was Dempsey's only true friend.

The tailor walked into the room ahead of Dempsey, his short cropped hair covering the forever receding hairline. A pair of small glasses balanced on his nose. As he quickly walked through the doorway, a slight limp was visible, a gift from the Nazis.

The room they had entered was huge. It was at least one hundred feet long and sixty feet wide. At one end of the room was a small shooting gallery, and the rest of it was a mass of crates, cases, and firearms. Cohen had always said, "If you want it, I can get it." Dempsey believed that statement because he had never been disappointed. Dempsey set down the holdall and paid attention to the aged arms dealer.

"Now Johnny, do you still carry that colt Python .357 everywhere with you?" questioned Cohen.

"Everywhere, Bernie." Dempsey patted the weapon under his jacket.

"Yours has the two and half inch barrel, doesn't it?" asked the Jew, who got a nod from the hitman. "Well, have a look at this. This is a Colt Python with an eight-inch barrel. A little more accuracy, you know." The tailor-come-arms-dealer handed Dempsey the weapon. The Colt weighed around two pounds, but Dempsey handled it as though it weighed only one.

"Pop off a couple of shots, Johnny. It's already loaded."

Dempsey liked the feel of the gun and accepted the offer.

They both walked towards the small shooting range and picked up a pair of ear protectors. After positioning the protectors carefully on his head, Dempsey raised the gun and cocked it. It did feel comfortable, but he still preferred the smaller barreled version. Fifty feet in front of him was the target of a man. Holding the weapon with both hands, Dempsey aimed at the small black circle on the torso of the target. With a gentle squeeze, the Colt Python .357 emitted a large bang, and Dempsey's hands recoiled upwards. The black circle now had a small hole in it.

"Try another, Johnny," insisted the arms dealer. Dempsey repeated the procedure, and, again, a deafening noise came from the weapon. The black circle now had a second hole in it. Dempsey's expression showed that he was impressed.

"Not bad, Bernie, but I'll stick with what I've got, thanks," remarked Dempsey with a sorry-sounding tone in his voice.

"I've something else for you to look at. Just hang on there, will you?" Cohen hurried towards a small cupboard on the wall. Before Dempsey could survey the room, Cohen was on his way back towards him.

"Now this you'll love," promised the Jew. In his hand was a large automatic handgun, which he promptly gave to Dempsey along with a clip of bullets.

"This, Johnny, is the Desert Eagle. This is the .44 Magnum version. It weighs three pounds, four ounces, and takes a seven shot clip. Here, try it."

Dempsey took the weapon and immediately noticed the difference in weight compared to the Colt Python. The tailor gestured to the shooting gallery As Dempsey approached the small range, he banged in the clip and pulled back the chamber.

"Most pistols are effective at around sixty metres. The weapon you are holding is accurate to around two hundred meters."

Dempsey's astounded look was enough to show he was impressed. He raised the automatic to the target with both hands. The index finger of his right hand gently squeezed the trigger. On that touch the weapon sprang into life, causing Dempsey's hands to react to the recoil. Keeping control of the automatic pistol, Dempsey kept his finger on the trigger until all seven shots had finished. The smell of cordite and smoke lingered in the air as Dempsey inspected the empty weapon in his hand.

Cohen looked at him and then at the target. Where the small black circle was, there was now a six inch in diameter hole. Cohen returned his attention to his friend.

"I can see you're impressed, my boy."

"This is one dangerous fucking gun, Bernie," replied Dempsey, still astounded at the ferocity of the weapon that he was holding.

"If you want it, it's yours."

"How can I turn it down?" responded the assassin.

"Johnny, it's yours, as a gift."

Dempsey nodded gratefully.

"Now then it's time for business. What was it you had in mind?" asked Cohen

"I need a rifle and scope, Bernie, for a big hit."

"Day or night?"

"Probably night."

"From how far?"

"Not sure, maybe three hundred metres."

"I've got the very thing," said Cohen. "Have a look at this over here." Dempsey followed the tailor from one side of the room to the other. Cohen stopped at a large cupboard, opened it, and retrieved a rifle from it. The weapon was extremely long and very elegant.

"This should be ideal, Johnny." The small Jewish man handed Dempsey the rifle so he could get a feel of it. "This is a semi-automatic Galil Sniper, twenty-five shot magazine and very accurate." Cohen sounded like a salesman. The assassin continued to inspect the weapon.

"Heavy, isn't it?" exclaimed Dempsey.

"About six and a half kilos. The telescopic sight on there is special."

"What's so special about this, then?"

"That, my boy, is a light-intensifier telescopic sight. On a moonless night, this will give you a shot of three hundred and fifty meters," explained Cohen.

Dempsey raised the gun to a firing position in order to get the feel of such a large weapon. "Feels good, Bernie. I'll take it."

"A very wise choice, Johnny." Replied the tailor, taking the gun, breaking it down, and putting each piece in an already prepared sports bag.

"Money in the usual way, Bernie?" asked Dempsey, already knowing the answer.

The small Jewish tailor nodded with a smile on his face. "The handgun is in the bag with plenty of ammunition for both weapons."

"Thank, Bernie," replied Dempsey as Cohen handed him the bag.

"Now you be careful, my boy, and I mean that," said the tailor.

Dempsey replied with a wink of his left eye and headed for the way out.

Graham Miller glanced at the clock on the office wall, five-fifty-five. Miller, like most of his fellow officers in the room, had had only a few hours sleep in the last two days. He was beginning to feel it. His attention was attracted by the office door opening, and Peter Grant entering.

"Sorry I'm late, people, call of nature."

The room was hot and full of cigarette smoke, coming mainly from DC Short, who was usually on sixty a day. Also in the room was Maggie Thomas, who was devouring a cheese sandwich in record time.

All three officers took notice as Grant began to speak. "So what information have we gathered so far? Maggie?" The woman constable referred to her notebook. "Brian Williams met Lomax around nine forty-five, Thursday morning. They played golf as normal, something they've done for the last ten years every Thursday. Lomax was in good spirits after playing very well."

"What about Williams, anything on him?" asked the senior officer.

"Law-abiding citizen, popular businessman, no form, no nothing, sir."

"Anything else, Maggie?"

Thomas referred to her notebook again. "Some witnesses at the golf club say they spotted a red Sierra parked near the entrance to the club. It apparently had the bonnet up, and there was a guy sitting inside. Only a vague description, though. There were traces of red paint found on Lomax's Mercedes, maybe a tie in there, sir."

"Good stuff. Check out local garages and car rental firms, it may lead us to a name or a better description. Graham, what have you got?" pressed the detective inspector.

Miller changed position in his chair. "Nothing big time on James Lomax. Only thing on his record was a warning for possession of cannabis. And that was six years ago. As for who would prosper from Lomax's death, well they all would in a way. June Lomax obviously keeps the house and estate, James Lomax continues to run the business, and Tina Lomax carries on at university. Really there is no difference, except that there is no more Charlie Lomax."

"Right. Follow up this red Sierra lead and see what comes of it," stated Grant. Then he looked at Short. "Brian, you go and see June Lomax, try and find out if there's been any family rifts lately. There was a house keeper there, have a chat with her as well, and for Christ's sake, be tactful. Okay, let's go."

Short and Thomas filed out of the room, leaving the sergeant and his superior.

"Guv, we've got fuck-all to go on. We need a breakthrough quick."

"I know, Graham. Something'll come up, I'm sure of it," responded Grant.

Then both men left the office.

Chapter Six

John Dempsey poured another glass of Jack Daniel's and replaced the bottle in its position on the cabinet. When planning a hit, he always listened to Guns 'n' Roses; somehow the loud music made him concentrate. As he sat down, the group's version of "Live and Let Die" began.

> When you were young and your heart
> was an open book, you use to say live
> and let live.

Dempsey opened the envelope and withdrew the contents. Inside was a photo of James Webster, and a list of various addresses. One was the address of Webster's home, another concerned a business interest, and several others were places Webster frequently visited. There was a list of appointments, up to and including the conference in thirteen day's time.

> Say live and let die.

Dempsey sipped at the bourbon and studied the photograph of the foreign secretary.

What have you got on the prime minister? Enough to have you killed, that's what, Dempsey thought. He took another sip of the bourbon and swallowed hard.

> What does it matter to you? When you've
> got a job to do...

Half a million pounds and that's it, no more killing, no more death, no more pain, and no more anger. France would be a nice place to live, or Canada. Dempsey rested his head back and closed his eyes. Soon he was asleep.

Say live and let die.

"Just shut the fuck up, will you? You fucking winging cunt." Chang slapped the woman around the back of the head, causing her to cry even more.

"What do you want with us? We've done nothing to you!" screamed the woman as she held on to her hysterical daughter. Chang pointed the 9mm Browning at them both.

"I said shut the fuck up, or don't you understand fucking English?" ranted Chang. Chang's mood was not good to say the least. He was irritable and agitated. The woman realised that pushing the intruder too far might not be a good idea. The girl became even more hysterical, so the woman embraced her even tighter.

Chang looked at his watch. He should have received the call by now. He was edgier and more nervous than ever. This was not going according to plan at all. If he had to kill them he would, but that was not part of the plan, either.

Chang heard a noise; it came from the front door area. Chang anxiously pointed the Browning at the living room door. As the living room door opened, he pulled the young girl by the hair from her mother's arms, causing the mother to topple backwards.

"What's going on, Chang?" asked Dempsey.

"I'm here for insurance, John. Rumour had it you were going to back out," said Chang.

The woman began to get up but was back on the ground after receiving a crack on the head from Chang's weapon. Dempsey's initial reaction was to go for the chinaman, but he retreated when the Browning returned to his daughter's head.

"The job's done Chang, let them go," said Dempsey as he put his hand inside his coat.

"I'm waiting for confirmation, John. Until then I'm not moving." Chang pushed harder and harder against the back of the girl's head, and Dempsey could not wait any longer. From under his jacket, he whipped out the Colt Python and pointed it at Chang. The woman began to scream, as did the girl.

"Let her go, Chang, I fucking mean it," roared Dempsey.

"Confirmation, John, that's all I need."

"Let her go, Chang. The job's been done!" repeated Dempsey. Chang began to smile in a chilling way.

"Okay, John, you win." Chang released his grip on the girl, who started to run towards her father. As she did, Chang pointed the Browning at the girl, and Dempsey saw what was coming but could do nothing.

"No!" cried Dempsey as the shot came from Chang's weapon.

Dempsey sat up, hearing the sound of the glass break as it hit the floor. That dream, that same fucking dream. The perspiration was pouring down Dempsey's face, mingling with his tears. Dempsey sat forward and clasped his hands over his face.

On the table in front of him was the newly acquired Desert Eagle pistol. Still crying, he picked up the firearm and took off the safety catch. Through watery eyes, he could see the photograph on the mantelpiece of Carole and Lisa, his wife and daughter.

Dempsey's gaze returned to the firepower in his hands. It would be so easy to join them. Just put the barrel under your chin and put the trigger, he thought. Better still in your mouth, won't miss then, will you? The bullet will go straight through your brains, and you won't know a thing about it.

Dempsey put the gun in his mouth and fingered the trigger. Again he saw the photograph on the mantelpiece. He removed the gun from his mouth and put the safety catch back on, then pounded his head with it three times, ignoring the pain he was causing himself. The only pain he felt at the moment was inside.

Dempsey threw the gun on to the coffee table in front of him and put his hands to his head. He couldn't kill himself. Others yes, himself no. He owed Carole and Lisa more than that. That night Dempsey went to bed drunk and in pain.

Chapter Seven

For most people to be summoned by the home secretary would be quite a worrying thing. Leonard Chalmers, though, had an idea why he was being summoned. Chalmers had received the call at eleven that morning; although a busy man, he could not turn down the home secretary, so made his way to the gentleman's club in Westminster. A lot of the members of Parliament used this establishment rather than the bar at the House of Commons. It offered a bit more privacy.

On entering the club, Chalmers was greeted by a doorman who was dressed in a rather loud waistcoat and bow tie.

"I have a meeting with Peter Campbell, the home secretary."

"May I be of assistance, sir?" asked the doorman with a Cornish accent.

"Oh yes, please follow me if you will, sir," responded the doorman, who then began to walk off at a quite rapid pace. Chalmers followed, admiring the decor and doing well to keep up with the doorman.

They entered a room full of leather Chesterfield furniture. There were pictures on the wall of famous men in history. No women, though, noticed Chalmers. He recognised Nelson, Wellington, Churchill, and Montgomery, but in a place like this women as famous as Florence Nightingale and Margaret Thatcher just did not make the grade.

Sitting in a large, brown leather chair was Peter Campbell, reading *The Times*.

"Leonard, glad you could make it," said Campbell as he arose and offered his hand to Chalmers. Chalmers accepted the handshake and sat in a chair adjacent to Campbell.

"I trust it's not too early for a little drink, Leonard," said Campbell as he attracted the attention of a waiter. The waiter hurried over and asked for the order.

"Cognac okay, Leonard?"

Chalmers nodded thankfully.

"Two cognacs please, Tim."

Again the waiter hurried off, disappearing to another room.

"Now then Leonard, how are things going? Well, I hope," said Campbell, with a slight hint of a Scottish accent.

"Fine, home secretary. Our little problem will be sorted out very soon."

"Good. This chap Dempsey, he is the best, isn't he?"

"Undoubtedly," replied Chalmers as the waiter reappeared with the two cognacs on a small tray.

"Thank you, Tim," said Campbell with a smile at the young waiter. He then returned his attention to Chalmers.

"Dempsey can be a little unpredictable sometimes, but he'll get the job done, mark my words," said Chalmers.

"It's a shame he'll have to die then, isn't it?" stated Campbell as he sipped at his cognac. "I assume you've taken care of that as well."

"It is all in hand, home secretary. I have no worries whatsoever," retorted Chalmers. When the young waiter walked past once again, Chalmers noticed Campbell giving him a wink and a smile.

"That's good to hear, Leonard. There will be positions open soon for a man of your stature and intelligence. I will keep you in mind," stated the home secretary.

"What do you mean, soon?"

"The prime minister won't last that long with all these accusations flying around now, will he?"

Chalmers looked on confused. "That's why I thought Webster was the target, to stop any possibility of damage to the prime minister.

"Leonard, my dear fellow, besides the PM himself, only two people know what he has done. One is James Webster, the other is myself. And if Webster cannot use the information for political gain, then I shall," said Campbell. "When the information gets out, the PM will resign. The deputy prime minister will temporarily take over, then there will be an election for party leader. The winner should eventually become prime minister."

"How can you be sure of a victory? Surely others will run for it," said Chalmers.

"The deputy prime minister is seventy-three. These days, that's too old. Malcolm Jennings, the chancellor, has only the prime minister as a friend; he'll have no backing. Webster, sadly won't be with us. That leaves me, and I have it in confidence that I will be the man they want."

"You appear to have it all worked out, sir, to the finest detail."

"That is why your input is essential. Carry this off well, and you will be rewarded, I can assure you," affirmed Campbell. "The man in charge of MI-5 is a total imbecile. When I assume power, I'll need someone that I can trust, and that, Leonard, would be where you fit in."

"I will certainly be doing my best, home secretary," replied Chalmers.

Campbell gulped down the cognac and called over the waiter again. "And I am certain, Leonard, that your best will be good enough. Two more cognacs please, Tim."

"Of course, sir," replied the waiter. As he walked off Campbell gazed after him, smiling.

There were seven addresses on Dempsey's list. Each one to be frequented in the next ten days by James Webster. One of the addresses on the list was Webster's home address. Dempsey decided the hit would take place there in two day's time. Last time, he had hired a car, but this time, he would buy a cheap old banger. He had looked in the local newspaper and picked out a couple of possibilities: an Escort and a Fiesta.

Webster's home was in Hertfordshire which was not much of a drive, but Dempsey wanted everything planned to the last minute. He would get the car, leave today, and find a place to stay for a couple of nights. Case out Webster's house, then on Tuesday do the hit.

The last one. No more after this, just a life of peace and quiet.

The phoned chirped merrily in Chang's pocket before he answered it. "Hello, Robert Chang here."

"Robert, it's Leonard. Just ringing to tell you to get ready. Dempsey has just contacted me, and said the job will be done on Tuesday. After that, he's yours. Remember, Robert, no room for any fuck-ups. This is important, you understand." The tone of Chalmers voice was more somber than usual, and Chang noticed it.

"Okay, Lennie. Leave it with me," stressed Chang.

"Right. See you soon then, Robert, and remember what I said." Chalmers hung up.

Chang returned the mobile to his pocket. Soon Dempsey would be his. Three years of waiting for revenge had caused Chang to become a ruthless man. Many of the people he had killed he had imagined were Dempsey. Chang guzzled his wine and called to Luigi, who was drying some glasses. "Another wine in here, Luigi, will you? I'm celebrating."

Chapter Eight

Steve Lambert was late; in fact, it was the third time in four days that he was late. He was sure the sarge would have his bollocks this time. He looked at his watch; five past two. Yesterday he was only two minutes late and got bollocked. God knows what would happen today.

The young PC shut his locker and ran to the briefing room. On his entry, there was a large cheer from Lambert's fellow officers and a stern gaze from Sergeant Highland.

"Alright! Quiet, everybody. I'll see you afterwards, Lambert," said the grizzly voice of Sergeant Colin Highland.

Lambert replied with a disconsolate nod, knowing he was in trouble. He noticed some of the other officers smirking, so he gave them a sarcastic smile.

Sergeant Highland then continued, "Here, ladies and gents, is a photofit picture of our possible murder suspect." The small stack of paper diminished as the pile was passed around the group of officers. "Show the picture to the people on the streets, and let's hope we get some response."

"I know him," blurted out Lambert. All eyes in the room went to him. "You remember that bloke last week, Sarge, who beat up them two yobs? Well, when they refused to press charges, I thought I'd go and have a word with him. I'm sure it's him, and I'm sure there was a red Sierra outside the guest house where he was staying."

"You best see DI Grant straight away then, Lambert," ordered Highland.

Lambert continued to stand there, waiting for the sarge to continue.

"Now, Lambert," stressed Sergeant Highland.

"Right, Sarge. I'm on me way," replied Lambert. He hurried out of the room.

At last he was useful. Three years a copper now and still things weren't right for him. He had ambitions of becoming a great detective, but he was beginning to realise it wasn't as easy as all that. He had thought about chucking it in, but with a wife, a three-month-old baby, and a mortgage, the money was essential.

Grant's office was two flights up the stairs, and by the time Lambert got there, he was puffing a bit. After knocking on the door, he heard Grant tell him to come in. Lambert opened the office door to see Grant behind his desk.

"What can I do for you? Be quick, though, will you? I'm up to my neck in it," said the DI.

"This photofit picture, sir, the one of the suspect in the Lomax murder...I think I spoke to him the other day," remarked the young PC.

"Lambert, isn't it?" asked Grant, who had now taken notice a little more.

"Yes sir, Steven Lambert."

"Right then, Steven, tell me what you've seen," said Grant, who spotted Graham Miller passing his door. "Graham, come here a minute," he shouted.

Miller entered the room, surprised to see the young constable standing there.

"Okay then, Steven, carry on," said Grant.

"Well sir, last Wednesday we received a call from the King's Head. Two bikers had had the shit kicked out of them by this stranger. When we questioned the bikers, they refused to press charges, so after chatting to the pub landlord and the barmaid, I discovered the suspect was staying at one of the guest houses on Tiller Street. I thought I'd have a chat with him, tell him to be careful, watch out for revenge attacks...you know, that sort of thing." Lambert looked at Miller and then returned his gaze to the inspector. "Well, he said he was a salesman of some kind and was in town on business."

"And he fits the photofit?" asked Miller.

"Yes, he does."

"Right then, Lambert, can you give us a description better than what we've already got?" asked Grant.

"Yes, I think so," responded Lambert.

"Graham, take Lambert with you and get the description. Then get back to me, and we'll go down to the pub and the guest house," instructed the detective inspector.

The constable followed the detective sergeant out of the room, and Peter Grant sat back in his chair and clapped his hands together,

"We'll soon have you, you bastard," muttered Grant under his breath.

Dempsey was quite impressed with the car he had bought. He had followed up an advertisement in the local rag for the Ford Fiesta that he was now driving. It was twelve years old, had seventy-five thousand on the clock, and a years MOT; not bad for four hundred quid.

From the information Dempsey had, Webster would be at his house in a place called Aston, just outside Stevenage in Hertfordshire. Apparently quite a plush house in the country, with some stables and a fair bit of land.

James Webster was fifty-one, married with two children, and relatively successful outside politics. Although he was the director on the boards of three major companies, most of his wealth was inherited. Webster's father had died when he was young, leaving his son a substantial amount of money, which Webster had successfully invested after consulting a financial advisory group.

Webster's political dreams had started thirty years ago when he attended a young conservatives' meeting. At the meeting, he made quite an impact and won a lot of supporters. Within three years, he was an MP—one of the youngest ever and already winning many admirers. Margaret Thatcher had tipped him as a future leader.

His first senior position was as minister for education in the last years of the so-called Iron Lady. He won promotion to the post of defense minister after her demise. The prime minister soon noticed how well Webster handled himself in some foreign affairs; thus his position now of foreign secretary.

Webster was a very ambitious man, and the prospect of being prime minister—no matter how he got there—was forever in his mind. He was given the damning information on the PM from a journalist friend who contacted him. Foolishly, he had confided in Campbell about the information and decided to reveal all in a bid to oust his leader. Although the prime minister was a good friend, friendship could not stand in the way of Webster's political ambition. His only mistake was confiding in Campbell, a man who had even more ambition than Webster.

As Dempsey continued his journey on the road of boredom, he was planning every step that he must tread. This was the most dangerous and most important assignment he had ever been asked to undertake; therefore there was no room for mistakes. One small fuck up could be the end for him, and he knew it. Further down the road, Dempsey caught sight of his next turn off. It would not be long now.

The King's Head was practically empty when Grant and his sergeant entered. Except for two men at the bar, the place was unoccupied. Behind the bar was Frank Wilson, the landlord. Grant and Miller glanced at each other, both taken aback by his hair, if it was his.

As they got nearer the bar, they were greeted by Wilson. "Afternoon gents, what can I get you?"

"My name is Peter Grant, Detective Inspector Peter Grant," stated Grant as he produced his warrant card from his pocket. "This is Detective Sergeant Miller. We were wondering if you could help us."

"Certainly, what's the problem then, officer?" replied Wilson with a smile.

"Last week there was a fracas of sorts involving a man and a couple of bikers," said Grant. "Could you describe the man?"

"About five feet ten, well-built. I think there was a scar over his left eye. Hang on, I'll call Susan—she served him his food. She might remember him." Wilson disappeared into a back room.

"Pretty much the same as Lambert's description, sir," commented Miller. Wilson reappeared with a pretty young woman from the room behind the bar.

"You remember that bloke who beat up Jimmy, don't you, Susan?" asked Wilson.

"Yeah, good looking bloke. Didn't say much, just hello and thanks," said the young barmaid.

"Did you notice his mood—was he nervous, calm, agitated?" asked Miller.

"Calm at first, then he went mental. Jimmy and his mate didn't mean anything when they had a go at him. He just exploded," replied Susan Potter.

Grant was about to continue when Wiggy spoke. "Very quick, though," interrupted the landlord. "He looked like he knew how to handle himself the way he went through them two."

"What do you mean by that?" queried Grant

"It just all looked very professional, as though he had been trained for it," said the landlord. Grant glanced at his sergeant, who was busy scribbling in his note book.

"You've both been very helpful, thank you," said Grant. The landlord nodded at Grant as he and Miller turned for the door.

"Any time, officers," shouted Wilson, a ridiculous smile still on his face.

The rain had started to come down just as they left the pub.

"What do you reckon, Guv? Army, maybe," said Miller as they approached their car.

"Could be any of the armed forces, even an ex-copper. Lambert said his name was Bob Johnson, didn't he?"

"I checked it out, Guv. No Bob Johnson matched the description."

"If he did Lomax, the chances are he would have used a false name, anyway. He's got to be the same man, I'm positive. You go round the B and B, see what the owner says. I'm going back to the factory to see if Maggie's come up with any more," said Grant. He opened the car door and began to climb into the car.

"But Guv, it's pissing down. I'm gonna get soaked."

"Graham, stop being a tart and get on with it."

As Miller looked on, Grant drove away in the Mondeo. Miller raised his collar up around his neck and began to mumble curses as he headed for the bed and breakfast.

Chapter Nine

Dempsey needed somewhere to stay while in Aston, so the sign he read as he passed the pub was just the ticket. He usually stayed at bed and breakfasts, hotels, or pubs. Once he even bought an old Volkswagen van and slept in it.

The former soldier parked his newly acquired blue Fiesta in the pub car park, noticing a sign saying for patrons only. As he looked at the pub, he wondered if there would be any room, as it was so small. If there wasn't, he would have to try somewhere else.

Dempsey grabbed the holdall which was beside him and then reached to the back seat for the attache' case which contained the Galil sniper rifle that had been dismantled. After locking his car door, he looked at his watch. It was just before ten. The pub would not be open, so he headed for the door at the side of the pub.

On reaching the door, Dempsey pushed the button for the doorbell with his free hand. The door opened almost immediately, revealing a dark-haired woman probably in her early forties. The first thing that caught Dempsey's eye was the low-cut blouse that she was wearing.

"I saw the sign for a room and wondered if one was still available," said Dempsey, his gaze again going to her chest.

"Yes love, there is a room free. Come in," replied the woman. Dempsey stepped inside, and she closed the door behind him. "It's fifteen pounds a night, that's with a breakfast and an evening meal. Will you be staying long?"

"Probably a couple of nights, that's all."

"I'll show you the room. This way," she said, beginning to climb the stairs. Dempsey noticed how short her skirt was and began to follow her up the stairs, admiring the view as he climbed. At the top, she opened the first door on the right and entered, with Dempsey in tow.

The room was small. It contained a bed, a small wardrobe, and a bedside cabinet. At the end of the bed on a wall bracket was a portable television.

"This will be fine, just perfect," remarked Dempsey who again found himself looking at the woman's ample chest. "I'll pay up front if that's okay."

"That's fine by me, love. Two nights, you say?"

Dempsey nodded in reply.

"Thirty quid then, darling," she said. Dempsey took out his wallet and removed three ten pound notes, then handed them to her.

"By the way, my name's Beryl. If you need anything, just shout. I'll let you know what dinner will be and what time later on, okay?"

Again Dempsey nodded in reply.

"I didn't catch your name, love. Gotta call you something, haven't I" asked Beryl.

"Oh sorry, it's Frank, Frank Corbett."

"Well pleased to meet you, Frank, here's a key for the door. The bathroom's just down the way if you wanna clean up. The bar'll be open in half hour. Pop down and have one on the house," said Beryl, then she shut the door behind her as she left.

Dempsey took the key and gently pushed it into the lock and turned. He hoped the sound of the latch snapping across would not draw any attention to him. After slipping quietly inside, he opened the holdall which he had placed on the bed, but still had the sight of Beryl's chest in his head. Dempsey could not help but smile as he removed his jacket, then the Desert Eagle pistol along with the holster.

Sod it, one drink's not going to cause any harm, is it? May even help with my cover. The view probably won't be bad, either. Dempsey continued smiling

It did not take Dempsey long to find Webster's house. He had had one drink in the pub (getting to know Beryl in the process) then left to find the country home of the foreign secretary.

As soon as Dempsey saw the size of the house, he knew he might have a problem. The house was set in fifty acres of land, most of which was surrounded by trees and hedgerows. With the stables and barns and some other small buildings nearby, there was a fair amount of lighting. Finding a spot to do the hit from would not be easy. He had to find a suitable place to enter the grounds without being seen and without attracting attention. As he drove past the thick,hedgerow he noticed a small gap—big enough to get through but not readily noticeable. As the car slowed while passing the grounds, the rain continued to fall. The Fiesta's wipers flicked from one side to another; their rubbing sound was all Dempsey could hear.

Dempsey slowed and pulled nearer the hedgerow, the Fiesta's wheels sliding in the mud. If anyone stopped him, he'd just make up some story. After getting out of the car, he walked over towards the gap he had spotted, then looked up and down the small road to ensure there were no prying eyes.

Dempsey just managed to squeeze through, and found the view for which he was looking. About two hundred and fifty yards away, the house stood in all its glory. In his pocket there was a pair of small binoculars. He took them out and fiddled with them until they were correctly focused. Looking through them, he had an excellent view of the house.

"Fuck me," whispered Dempsey. Standing at the window was James Webster, there, ready to be hit. If it had been at night, Dempsey would have done him there and then, but he had to wait. He'd do the hit tonight and get it over with; then, he could get on a plane and go where he wanted.

Chapter Ten

> Feels like I'm knocking on heaven's door.
> – Bob Dylan

Dempsey returned to the pub around three, had a nap, and then ate a meal cooked by Beryl. The time was six-thirty now.

Have a beer then leave about seven, he thought. Carry out the hit hopefully by nine.

There were already quite a few people in the bar, which surprised Dempsey. As he walked through the bar area, Beryl gave him a wink, and Dempsey responded with a smile.

"What'll it be then, Frank?" asked the landlady. Dempsey almost forgot that his name was now Frank, and he hesitated before he answered.

"Pint of lager please, Beryl," said Dempsey. Beryl then walked down the bar a little way to get Dempsey's drink from the pump.

"I hear you're staying with us for a couple of nights, then." The voice caught Dempsey by surprise, as he did not know the man who spoke to him.

"That's right, Frank Corbett," Dempsey held out his hand, which was shaken by the man next to him.

"Bill Ross. You already know the wife, Beryl, don't you?"

"Pleased to meet you. Your wife certainly knows how to cook," said Dempsey, pretending to be friendly.

"That she does, Frank. I can call you Frank, can I?"

"That's my name," replied Dempsey.

Beryl was returning with his lager.

"I see you've met Bill, then. One-ninety please, love," she said.

Dempsey gave her two pound coins and began to sip at his drink as Beryl went to the cash register.

"What brings you to Aston, Frank?" asked Ross.

"Business. I'm meeting a chap later to finalize a few things."

"What business are you in then, Frank?" continued Ross.

"I'm a salesman for a firm that manufactures carrier bags. Hopefully the chap I'm seeing will bring some money my way," said Dempsey, continuing with the lie.

"So where are you from originally, then? London?" asked Ross.

Dempsey wondered if this was Twenty Questions. Beryl, who had been listening, interrupted. "Bloody hell, Bill, give him a chance, will you?"

"Sorry Frank, force of habit, I suppose. Used to be a copper, retired last year and bought this place," said Ross.

Dempsey looked at him again, sipping at his pint. He couldn't believe it. Here he was talking complete crap, about to terminate the life of the foreign secretary, and staying in the same house as an ex-copper.

"Was you in the job long, Bill?" asked Dempsey, trying to make conversation, but not really wanting to continue.

"Eighteen years. Made sergeant, you know."

"You don't look old enough to retire."

"Got stabbed by a little shit one night, and lost one of me lungs, so they pensioned me off. We sold our house and got a good deal on this place," stated Ross. For one moment Dempsey felt some kind of sympathy for this man standing next to him.

"Want another, Frank?" asked the former police sergeant.

Dempsey looked at the clock on the wall. It was almost six-fifty.

"Best not. I'm driving to that meeting I've got, don't wanna get pulled, do I?" said Dempsey.

Bill Ross laughed heartily, almost choking on the half of bitter he was drinking. "If you're back late, just ring the doorbell. Someone'll be up."

"Cheers, Bill. Hopefully I won't be too late," replied Dempsey, who began to make his way back to his room.

When Dempsey got back to his room, he locked the door after he entered. He opened the attache' case to check his rifle one last time. Everything was in order, so Dempsey closed the case, then reached for the sports holdall. From it, he took the Desert Eagle pistol, which was still in the holster, and positioned it around his shoulders so it fitted snugly under his left armpit. Again he fished in the holdall and pulled out the seven shot magazine. After removing the pistol, he slammed in the magazine and returned it to its position under his arm.

He was ready, ready for the biggest test of his life, and if he passed, that would be it—off to wherever he wanted, with a new life and a new start.

Dempsey put on his leather jacket and checked that he had his mobile phone. After satisfying himself that he was ready, he left for Webster's house, knowing this would be the most important night of his life.

James Webster had gotten home around six, after a pressing day in parliament. He had attended various meetings all day, and had to be present at question time in the House of commons, where his party leader and prime minister was again being run through the mill.

When he got home, he showered and mentally ran through several papers for the following day. At seven-thirty, he decided to call it a day and enjoy the rest of the evening with his wife.

The foreign secretary poured himself a large whiskey and splashed it with soda. As he eased himself into an armchair, his wife of twenty-five years entered the room.

"Hard day, darling?" she said, smiling.

"You could say that. Want one?" replied Webster, raising his glass.

"Only a small one for now, Jim. Don't forget Tom and Alice are coming round for dinner. You best get changed."

"I totally forgot. What time will they be here?" inquired Webster, who was now pouring a small whiskey for his wife.

"Around eight-thirty! Jim, how could you forget? We arranged it last week."

"Slipped my mind. Anyway, there is still plenty of time," responded the foreign secretary. "Cheers."

Webster had just handed his wife the glass when the first bullet hit him. The first thing Louise Webster heard was the splinter of glass, then she saw that her husband had one hand on his throat with blood erupting over his fingers.

The second hit Webster in the side of the head, causing a large piece of skin to flap open as blood streamed from the wound. Webster was already dead, but before he finally collapsed, a third bullet struck.

This caught him in the back of his head causing devastating damage. Due to him falling forward as the bullet struck, the exit wound was at the top of his forehead. Pieces of brain and skull splattered Louise Webster, who was screaming hysterically. Webster crashed in a heap on the floor, his bowels already collapsed, his head a bloody mess of pink and grey matter.

Dempsey did not bother to break down the gun; instead he ran. The rain continued to lash down, making the ground a little unsteady underfoot. Dempsey knew Webster was dead and there would be no need to follow up.

After exiting through the small gap in the hedgerow, Dempsey raced to his car, which was hidden about two hundred yards away. Checking behind him for cars (or anything for that matter), Dempsey forced himself to remain calm. If he looked suspicious, then it could jeopardize the whole operation.

On reaching the car, he opened the boot, positioned the rifle in it, and closed it down firmly. Now he was beginning to really calm down, and he walked to the driver's side of the car and opened the door. Within seconds, the car was revved up, and Dempsey pulled away, being careful to watch the speed. He did not want to make a mistake now. The lights of the Fiesta lit the road up, seemingly brighter than normal. Dempsey thought it was probably some psychological illusion just making him feel paranoid.

Now that the job had been completed, Dempsey could leave and get right out of the assassination business. As soon as he got to the pub, he would telephone Chalmers and tell him the job had been carried out. Then as soon as the money appeared in his account, he would withdraw every penny he had and head for France. No more killing, no more death, and no more pain.

Dempsey arrived back at the pub around eight forty-five. On the way back he had stopped and disassembled the Galil sniper rifle and repositioned it in the attache' case. He had also changed his shoes, because the others were caked in mud.

After entering the pub, Dempsey was met with a greeting from Bill Ross, who had now found his way to the working side of the bar. "All sorted out Frank?" Ross bellowed.

"Yes, thanks, Bill," replied Dempsey. "Pour us a pint, will you? I'll be back in a minute."

Dempsey went through the bar and up the stairs to his room, locking the door after entering. He put the case on the bed and took out the mobile phone from his jacket. After punching several numbers, he heard the ring.

"Hello, Leonard Chalmers speaking."

"Chalmers, it's Dempsey. The job's done."

"Excellent job, John. And way ahead of schedule. When will you be back?"

"Sometime during the night. Just get my money sorted out," snarled Dempsey.

"Has there ever been a problem before? Leave it with me. I'll call you tomorrow."

"Remember, Chalmers, that's it. I'm retired now, that was part of the deal."

"I remember, John...this was your last assignment. We'll talk more tomorrow." Chalmers hung up. Dempsey frowned, wondering what it was that would have to wait until tomorrow. He decided he needed that pint now.

Robert Chang was in the shower when Chalmers called. Chang had just spent most of the day with a girl, taking her to his wine bar and then getting stoned on cocaine. After having sex with her, he had snorted some more.

He often went with high class hookers, and each time the same thing happened: the winebar, snorting coke, and then sex. Chang had little respect for women, often abusing them and on some occasions even resorting to rape to please his sexual fetishes.

On this occasion, though, he was in one of his good moods, and just straight sex had been enough. He met the girl through an agency; they recommended the blonde, busty Carla to him, and he phoned her and they had arranged to meet. At a thousand pounds a go, she was far from cheap, though.

Chang heard the phone ringing and got out of the shower, putting a towel around his waist as he walked to the bedroom. Carla was on the bed, giggling, the cocaine still in her body and still on her body. Traces of the white powder remained on her breasts. When she reached for the mobile phone and pressed the receive call button, Chang snatched it from her hand and pushed her back onto the bed.

"Fucking leave it, you stupid bitch," he shouted. This only caused her to giggle more and annoy Chang. The Oriental put the phone to his ear. "Who is it?"

"It's Chalmers. Dempsey's yours, okay?"

As Chalmers spoke, the prostitute ran her hand up the inside of Chang's towel, her fingertips brushing his penis.

"Consider it done, Leonard."

Both men hung up.

"Come on, Robert, fuck me again," said Carla, who had now taken Chang's penis firmly in her hand.

Chang shook his head. "Business to attend to. Get dressed."

"Come on, ten minutes," insisted Carla, stroking Chang's manhood.

"I said get dressed," snapped Chang, hitting the prostitute in the face. Carla fell back with blood seeping from her bottom lip. Chang looked at the hooker, who was now cowering up against the wall.

"Now, please, get dressed," said Chang. This time Carla did as she was told.

Dempsey had returned to the bar at nine-fifteen, but what he had done that night was only just sinking into his mind. For money, he had terminated the life of the foreign secretary. What a shitty way to make a living. It was the only thing Dempsey was any good at.

He could not stay in the pub too long, because tomorrow the whole area would be swarming with police and who-knows-what government departments will be asking questions. He decided he would leave during the night, and drive back to London. He would see Bernie Cohen in the morning, return the rifle, say his good-byes, and then he could leave for France.

The pub was gradually emptying, people wanting to get home before it got too cold, or because they had to get up for work in the morning.

"Another pint, Frank?" asked Beryl Ross.

"Just a half, please, Beryl," replied Dempsey.

The television that was up high in the corner suddenly became the centre of attention as a newsflash began.

"Turn the sound up," someone shouted from the back of the pub as the newsreader began to relay the story.

"The foreign secretary, Mr. James Webster, was shot dead this evening at his home in Hertfordshire."

Bill Ross turned to Dempsey, his face shocked by the news. "Fucking hell, he only lived up the road."

"What, near here?" responded Dempsey, trying to seem shocked by the news. The newsreader continued to chat away as people returned to their drinks.

"...his wife is being comforted by friends. We'll bring you more information on our main news at ten."

Beryl Ross was approaching with the half lager that Dempsey had ordered. "Poor woman, having that happen in front of her."

"Bill said it was only up the road," said Dempsey, continuing the charade.

"Nice woman, Mrs. Webster, and Mr. Webster come to that."

"Did you know them, then?"

"When we opened this place, they came along as special guests. What a shame."

Dempsey looked at the landlady as she spoke. She really was very sorry, which only made Dempsey feel even more guilty about what he had done that evening.

"Hope you've got a good alibi, Frank," interrupted Bill Ross.

"What?" said Dempsey seriously. "You don't think it was me, do you?"

"Just pulling your leg, Frank," said Ross, chuckling. Dempsey failed to see the funny side of the joke and began to guzzle the half pint.

"I best be off to bed, I think. All this traveling just tires me out," said Dempsey, as he finished off his drink.

"Sure you can't force another?" asked Beryl.

"No thinks, I've got a little bit of paperwork to do, anyway." Dempsey headed for his room, wondering how serious Bill Ross was being. As an ex-copper, Ross might put two and two together. At three in the morning Dempsey left for London.

Detective Inspector Peter Grant was still at the station when he heard the news of James Webster's death. He thought little of it, except for poor bastard. With him in the office was Sergeant Graham Miller.

"Get that updated description to all the television channels ready for the morning."

"Right, Guv," replied Miller. "We are gonna get this bastard, aren't we?"

"I don't know, Graham. It's been a few days now and all we've got is that photofit. He may be ex-forces, he may be an ex-copper. Let's hope that description brings us something."

Miller could see that his senior officer did not look too hopeful.

"You best get on Graham. Janet will be wondering where you are," said Grant. Miller nodded and left for home. Grant would not see his family for another two hours.

Chapter Eleven

Dempsey was back at his flat in London by four-thirty in the morning. He had left the pub in Aston without waking anyone, and had driven straight home.

He managed two hours sleep but, as always, found it hard to sleep after a hit. By seven he had showered and dressed, and was undecided about having breakfast. Still undecided, he turned on the television.

The seven-thirty news was still on, and the shooting of James Webster was the lead story. The reporter on the screen looked cold and tired, and as she spoke into the microphone, rain began to fall upon her. Dempsey turned up the volume to listen to what she had to say.

"At around seven-thirty yesterday evening, the foreign secretary was fatally shot. James Webster was struck by three bullets, two of them head wounds. He was alone with his wife, expecting dinner guests, when the shooting happened. Louise Webster is said to be in a state of shock and has been heavily sedated. Police are refusing to comment, but terrorist organisations are thought to be responsible."

The screen then cut back to the newsreader in the studio; compared to the other reporter, he looked warm and glad that he was inside. He said the prime minister had just made a statement condemning the murder, saying it was a savage attack on a defenseless man. Dempsey shook his head at the hypocritical remarks coming from the leader of the government and sipped at the mug of tea he had in his hand.

The story continued on the news for most of the next half hour: members of parliament saying what a nice man Webster was; some condemning the shooting; others talking about the life of the former foreign secretary. It was all the usual hypocritical bullshit that politicians spouted when a so-called friend had died.

Dempsey got up and turned the television off, deciding to give Bernie Cohen a ring and find out when he could return the rifle. It was after eight, and Dempsey knew that Bernie wasn't the type who lay in bed. Bernie was usually up early to get the shop ready. After retrieving the mobile from his pocket, Dempsey punched in the relevant numbers and waited for the receiver to be picked up. After a few seconds, Dempsey heard the voice of his old Jewish friend.

"Hello, who is that?"

"Bernie, it's me, John Dempsey."

"Ah, Johnnie boy. What is the problem?" enquired the old man.

"I have some merchandise to return, Bernie. Will today be alright?"

"Yes, no problem. How about elevenish, okay?" answered Cohen.

"Eleven o'clock is fine with me. See you then."

"Was that you at work last night, Johnnie?" Cohen's voice had turned sorrowful, as though he disapproved of what had been done.

"Yes, I was at work last night," replied Dempsey. The answer was met with silence, so Dempsey continued. "See you at eleven, Bernie."

Still there was no response. Dempsey pressed the end-of-call button and wondered why his friend had not responded. This was obviously one hit of which Bernie had not approved. Dempsey finally decided to have some corn flakes and set about getting a bowl and milk.

Leonard Chalmers had been summoned to the home secretary's office at ten o'clock. The call had come through the previous day before the assassination had even happened.

The secretary showed Chalmers in to the office, where Peter Campbell, the home secretary, was positioned behind a huge wooden desk.

"Leonard, please, sit down."

Chalmers did as requested.

"A pot of coffee please, Muriel," ordered Campbell.

The secretary turned and left, closing the door behind her.

"Excellent job, Leonard. You've done well."

"Dempsey was always the best man for the job. I told you that from the start," retorted Chalmers.

"Indeed you did, Leonard. Now, when will the second stage of the operation be completed."

"I have a man on it already. He knows what to do and how important it is for him to succeed," replied Chalmers again, decisively.

The door then opened after a light knock, and the secretary entered with a tray.

"Thank you, Muriel," said Campbell. Again the secretary left. "Now then, Leonard, do you play golf at all?"

Chalmers found this a strange question but answered all the same. "Not for a while, don't always get the time. Why?"

"I've some friends for you to meet. Like I said, you get this job carried out correctly and discreetly, and there will be a place for you when I am prime minister. Now these chaps are all good friends, and I'd like you to meet them. I thought the golf course would be ideal. What do you say then, Leonard?" asked Campbell, pouring out the coffee for both of them.

"Okay, why not?" Chalmers splashed some milk in his coffee and then stirred it.

"We'll say next weekend then, shall we? By then we'll know exactly what is going on, won't we?"

Chalmers did not particularly like the way Campbell looked at him, but if there was going to be a decent job after all this then why not go along with him?

"I best brush up on my swing, then," stated Chalmers.

Peter Grant was not used to failing in a case; in fact, he never had. Every murder inquiry he had been in charge of had brought in a result. This time, though, Grant was skeptical. They had no real evidence and no real leads in the murder of Charles Lomax. Deep down Grant was beginning to believe that this case was going to beat him.

A knock at the door echoed throughout Grant's office.

"Come in," bellowed Grant. The door opened to show a young WPC standing there.

"Excuse me, sir, but there is a Detective Chief Inspector Collins to see you. Shall I show him in?"

Grant sat there, slightly stunned. What would the DCI want with him? "Yes, show him in, will you."

The next two or three minutes were left for Grant to wonder why he was to have the pleasure of a visit from the detective chief inspector.

"Here we are, sir," said the WPC as she directed the DCI into the room. Grant stood up and held out his hand to his senior officer, who responded by accepting the handshake.

"DI Peter Grant, sir. How can I help?"

"Pleased to meet you, Peter," said Collins with a Yorkshire accent. "I understand you're working on a murder case at the moment."

Grand responded with a nod of his head. "Please, take a seat, sir," said Grant, offering Collins a chair.

Collins sat down. "A professional hit of sorts, I understand," remarked Collins, his grey bushy moustache covering some of his mouth. A problem for lip-readers, thought Grant.

"That's right, one Charles Lomax, shot six times with an automatic weapon last week."

"How near are you to catching the killer?" asked Collins.

"Not much to go on, I'm afraid. We've released quite an accurate photofit today to the media. We hope that will bring something up."

"I take it you heard about the foreign secretary. Well, I'm in charge of that case, and I think there might be a link," said Collins. "Do you know where your man stayed while in town?"

"A small bed and breakfast," replied Grant. "We dusted the room and picked up a few prints. Some were untraceable. We also believe he could be, or was, in the forces."

"What makes you say that?" queried Collins.

"Our chap was supposedly in a fight in the local pub. As the barman put it, he handled himself like a professional. Our investigation that way has led to nothing, though."

"Okay Peter, this investigation is top secret. We think our man stayed at a pub, left during the night. We've got some prints, so we'll cross-check them with yours. The descriptions are almost identical; the way both men have worked also seems very much alike," said the DCI.

"So where do we go from here, are we off the case here or what?" demanded Grant.

"Far from it, Peter. Continue your investigation, tell only those who need to know. I'll be speaking with your superiors in a moment." Collins reached in his pocket and withdrew a card. "Here is my number at work and at home, if anything comes up give me a ring. There's a fax number on there as well, if you need to send any information."

Grant took the card and looked at it. Grant stood up and held out his hand.

"Good talking to you, Peter. Keep up the good work." After shaking hands with Grant, Collins opened and then disappeared through the door.

"Bollocks," shouted Grant. He was not going to let this case go now, not for Collins to come swanning in a grab all the glory, or for that matter any SIB wanker. Grant picked up the receiver of this telephone and prodded in a number. "Graham, get Maggie and Brian and come in my office, will you?" Grant did not wait for a reply as he slammed the receiver down.

There was nothing in the world Robert Chang wanted more than to kill Dempsey. For three years he had waited for the chance of retribution. Five months lying in a hospital bed with serious gunshot wounds had done little for Chang, except build up a lot of hatred.

After a little piece of investigating, he found out about Dempsey's old friend from when he was in the army, Bernard Cohen. If Cohen didn't know where Dempsey was, then no one would.

Chang parked his Porsche fifty yards or so from the small tailor's that was owned by Dempsey's friend. He locked the car door and headed for the entrance to the shop, dodging traffic as he jogged across the road. The rain made small patches on the Chinaman's expensive suit. It had been raining for three days now.

Cohen was in the back of the shop when he heard the bell ring, which signified the shop door being opened.

"Hang on, I'll be there in a moment."

Chang recognised the Jewish accent and smiled. When he had closed the door, he turned over the sign to show that the shop was now closed. He then knocked the latch across.

Cohen appeared from the back room, a tape measure around his neck.

"Now my friend, how can I help you?" asked the tailor, looking at Chang's Armani suit. "That's a very nice suit that you are wearing. I'm afraid I have nothing of that quality."

"I'm not here to be measured for a suit, old man. I want information."

"What kind of information?" asked Cohen, noticing the sign and the latch on the door. "What's going on, who are you?"

"That's not important. Tell me what I want to known and then I'll leave," responded Chang, moving slowly towards the elderly man.

"Who do you think you are, coming in here and talking to me like that? Go on, get the fuck out of my shop!" yelled Cohen.

Chang moved quickly, bringing his right hand through and ramming the punch into Cohen's face. Blood erupted from the nose of the old man as he fell backwards. Chang leaned over his prey.

"Now you little fucking Jew, where is John Dempsey?" snarled the Oriental. Cohen's hand was swamped in blood coming from his broken nose.

"Where is John Dempsey?" asked Chang again.

"Go fuck yourself," spat out the old man. Chang reached out and grabbed the tailor, dragging him to his feet. With two sickening punches to the stomach, Chang broke three of Cohen's ribs. Again Cohen slumped to the floor, gasping for breath.

"Now one more time, you sniveling little fuck, where is Dempsey?" Chang's patience was now almost nonexistent. Still Cohen writhed on the floor in pain, probably not even hearing the last question.

Chang withdrew a switchblade from his pocket and opened it to its full extent. He dragged Cohen to his feet once again. The blood that was pouring profusely from Cohen's nose had now covered most of his face.

"Right, Jew, I've tried to be nice and you haven't cooperated, so now I'll get nasty. For the last time, where is John Dempsey?"

Cohen was near to passing out, but in his mind memories of the war, when he was tortured, came flooding back. "Like I said, you slant-eyed bastard, fuck yourself," rasped the old man. They were to be his last words.

Chang grabbed the old man by the throat and thrust the knife into the side of the old man's head. The blade passed through Cohen's ear and went fully four inches in, cutting through the skull and entering the brain. Cohen collapsed to the floor. His body quivered, the nerves attempting to hold on for as long as they could. He eventually stopped shaking. Cohen was dead.

Chang bent down to retrieve his knife. He tugged at it, but it would not come free from Cohen's head. The Oriental then placed his foot on the dead tailor's face and again tugged at the knife. This time it came free, emitting a crack from where the skull had split. The blade was covered in blood and small pieces of grey globules.

Noticing the pieces of brain and blood on the blade, Chang wiped it on the old man's waistcoat, first one side, then the other. The Oriental looked at his victim and muttered, annoyed because he got no information from him. In anger he let fly with a series of kicks at the dead man's body. Ribs and other bones cracked under the intensity of the attack.

Chang stepped back from the body, closed the switchblade, and returned it to his pocket. He then straightened his jacket, checking to be sure there was no blood on it, and ran his hands through his dark black, shoulder-length hair.

In some ways happy with his work, Robert Chang was angry with himself. Letting his emotions get the better of him was a problem he often had. Many a person had died because he didn't bother to ask questions first.

Chang headed for the door, slipped the latch off, and exited, observing if anyone would see him leaving. He closed the door behind him and cantered across the road to his waiting Porsche. After unlocking the door and entering the car, he was ready to go, but it was then he noticed the blue Fiesta pull up outside the shop of the recently deceased Bernard Cohen.

The Chinese hitman recognized the occupant of the car as soon as he saw him; it was John Dempsey. Chang smiled, realising his visit was not a waste of time after all.

"So the old Jew was a freebie," said Chang.

Dempsey jumped out of the car, eager to see his old friend and tell him he was getting out of the country. As he approached the front door there seemed to be a spring in his step, as though a huge burden had been lifted from his shoulders. Then he noticed the sign read closed on the front door. Dempsey glanced at his Sekonda wrist watch. It was ten-fifty; perhaps Bernie had shut up the shop because he was expecting him. Carrying the attache' case containing the Galil rifle, Dempsey walked up to the front door and looked in through the glass. Everything looked alright, so Dempsey turned the door handle and entered the shop.

"Bernie? It's John, John Dempsey," shouted the assassin, waiting for a reply. Dempsey surveyed the shop, a frown on his face. Where was Bernie?

Dempsey took two steps forward, then he saw the body. He let the attache' case fall from his hand. All Dempsey could see was his friend's feet, the rest of his body hidden by the shop counter.

Any happiness that John Dempsey had in his body left him and turned to sorrow. As he approached the corpse, tears began to well up in his eyes because he knew that his friend was dead before he got to him.

It was only when he stood over his dead friend that he realised how maliciously Bernie had been murdered. The head wound was seeping blood, mixing with more of the red liquid that had begun to congeal around his face. There was a visible hole in the head, which the now grieving Dempsey guessed was the result of a screwdriver or a knife.

Dempsey held his hand to his head while the tears cascaded down his cheeks. In a fit of rage, Dempsey clinched his fists and threw a huge punch at the wall. The force of the punch would normally have hurt, but this had no effect on him. All of his pain was inside.

Dempsey again looked at his dead friend, wondering what he should do. Telephone the police—no, they would find Bernie's arsenal of weapons. Perhaps he should try to get rid of the body himself. It was risky but what else could he do?

It was then that the shop door opened, startling Dempsey. In front of him stood a middle-aged woman with a carrier bag in her right hand, containing a jacket. The woman stared at the hitman.

"Where's Mr. Cohen?" As she said it, she saw the body on the floor, then returned her stare to Dempsey.

"It's not what you think," said Dempsey determinedly. The woman let go a scream and bolted for the door. Dempsey followed but could not stop her from entering the street. Outside the woman shouted and screamed. Dempsey decided to go, but it was then that he saw the figure on the opposite side of the street staring at him.

Robert Chang went for the 9mm. Beretta under his arm. Dempsey, still amazed at the person he was looking at, realised Chang was going for a gun, and Dempsey ducked down, opening his car door in the same process.

The woman had attracted some attention now, and people were coming to see what the noise was all about. Dempsey finally managed to open the door when he heard the sound of the first shot.

The window in the passenger side shattered, the 9mm shell passing through it at great speed and hitting the old woman in the side, splintering her pelvic bone. As she collapsed to the ground, people now realised they could be in the line of fire and began to disperse.

Keeping as low as possible, Dempsey got in the driver's seat and retrieved his own gun from the holster under his jacket. Without looking where he was pointing the gun, Dempsey raised the Desert Eagle and fired off a round, forcing Chang to dive for cover. The 11.17mm slug slammed into the wall near Chang, making a huge hole in the brickwork.

Dempsey raised his head slightly, noticing Chang was on the ground. This might be his only chance, he thought. Quickly he started the ignition, put the car in gear, and released the handbrake. Dempsey floored the accelerator, and the wheels spun for a second on the wet tarmac before the Fiesta shot forward, snapping Dempsey's head and neck back. Chang saw what was happening and ran for his own car as people cowered on the ground.

As soon as he was in the Porsche, Chang floored the accelerator and began his pursuit. Weaving in and out of traffic, he passed cars to keep the Fiesta in sight. Chang drove like a man possessed, flooring the accelerator continuously and fighting to keep control of the car.

Dempsey, meanwhile, was getting everything he could from the Fiesta. As he screeched around a corner, an oncoming driver waved his fist in anger, only to see the red Porsche of Chang scream past moments later.

The German car was definitely gaining, and Dempsey knew it.

How was Chang alive?

Who had helped him?

How did he know where to find him?

These were just three of the questions going through Dempsey's head, but more important matters were apparent. In front of him, Dempsey spotted the traffic lights were red and cars were waiting. Braking and swerving the car, he mounted the pavement, narrowly avoiding a couple who were walking arm in arm. Then he swerved back, just missing a transit van.

Chang repeated the manouevre, except for grazing the transit with the back of his Porsche. Still following at high speed, Chang pointed and let off two shots from the Beretta in his right hand. The first blasted the wing mirror on Demspey's side. The second hit the back window and shattered the glass, some of which Dempsey felt hit him in the back of the head. A small hole appeared in the windscreen where the bullet exited. Dempsey tried to push himself lower into the seat, giving his pursuer less to aim for.

Still under his control, Dempsey swerved the Fiesta, first to the right then to the left, hoping to avoid any more gunfire. The Porsche continued to gain on the Fiesta, almost touching bumper to bumper. Again Chang let off two more shots. The first missed entirely, but the second just missed Dempsey, whose head turned as he saw a large hole appear in the passenger seat next to him.

Dempsey braked as he turned the corner, and the back of the car fishtailed on the slightly wet road. Chang, though, lost control, and the Porsche spun around on the same corner. Dempsey saw his chance and performed a text book emergency stop. He then slammed the car in reverse and headed for the Porsche, which had begun to move again.

Before Chang had moved even six feet, the Fiesta crashed into the Porsche. The impact sent Chang's head forward into the steering wheel, causing a slight cut on the bridge of his nose. For the first time, Dempsey had the upper hand and pointed the Desert Eagle pistol at the Porsche. Chang threw himself across the passenger seat, knowing what was coming.

Twisting himself around in the driver's seat, Dempsey let go three shots from the huge firearm in his hand. All three slammed into the windscreen of the Porsche, and splinters of glass showered the oriental hitman as he kept as low as possible.

As soon as the third shot had gone, Dempsey, who had kept the engine running, changed gear and accelerated away. The tyres burned and smoked as he screamed away.

Chang raised his head to see the Fiesta turning a corner up ahead. By now a crowd had begun to gather, an elderly man opened the door on the driver's side showing some sympathy as he spoke. "You alright mate? I saw it all if you need a witness for the police."

"Fuck off and mind your own business, you old piece of shit," growled Chang as he started the car up. The old man backed away, shocked by Chang's reaction.

"I'll have you next time, Dempsey," muttered the oriental as he pulled away. The sound of sirens could be heard vaguely in the background as the battered Porsche headed up the road.

Chapter Twelve

When Dempsey returned home, he broke down and cried about his friend who he had lost that day. Bernie Cohen, the only person who had really helped since Carole and Lisa were murdered, was now dead as well; all three murdered by that fucking Chinaman.

How was he alive?

Who told him about Bernie?

Who was helping him?

Just some of the questions that were going through Dempsey's head. None of which he knew the answers for.

Dempsey unscrewed the top off the Jack Daniel's bottle and swigged at it, grimacing as he swallowed, the liquid burning as it eased its way down Dempsey's throat. After what he had been through today, he needed a drink, and lots of it. But the television soon changed his mind about a drunken oblivious afternoon.

The screen showed a photofit picture, and Dempsey knew it was of him and turned up the volume. The picture disappeared, and a suit clad newsreader continued the story.

"This man is wanted for questioning for the murder of James Webster. He is also thought to be involved in the murder of a Kent businessman. Detectives have said not to approach him, as he maybe extremely dangerous. If you think you know or have seen this man, then call the phone number on the screen now."

Dempsey immediately picked up his mobile phone and punched in the numbers for Leonard Chalmers. Instead of Chalmers answering, though, all he got was a voice saying the number did not exist.

"Fucker," said Dempsey through gritted teeth. "The bastard's set me up." Dempsey ran his hand through his hair, looking around him at the same time.

He had to get out of it, before anyone informed him to the police. The picture likeness on the television was almost perfect; even the old, half-blind man next door would have recognized him. All airports and seaports would be staked out with police waiting for him. Dempsey had an idea and took a little red book from the drawer of the unit by the window.

He thumbed through the pages until he got the name and number for which he was looking. He again took the mobile phone and pressed a series of digits eager to hear the voice he sought.

"Hello, Jimmy Flynn here. Well I'm not here actually, I'm out at the moment, but if you could leave your name and message after the tone, I'll get back to you," said the voice with a slight Irish tint to it. The hitman waited for the tone and spoke as soon as he heard it.

"Jimmy, it's John Dempsey. I need to go to France tonight, discreetly if you know what I mean. You've got my number. Call me, as soon as possible, on my mobile," said Dempsey hurriedly, ensuring the whole message was recorded.

He didn't have much time, and he knew it. The assassin went to the bedroom and grabbed the sports holdall, which was on top of the wardrobe. He then put some clothes in the holdall—T-shirts, jeans, socks, and underwear were all that he needed for now. After switching the television off, Dempsey left.

The file that Chang had on Dempsey gave him only a few addresses where to find the former SAS man. The Cohen shop had been one such address. Chang glanced through the short list of addresses he had in front of him and chose one. If Dempsey was not there, he would pick an other, and so on, until he found him.

The Fiesta must have looked quite conspicuous with all the damage it had. The back window was missing, the windscreen had a hole in it, one of the wing mirrors was gone, and the rear of the car was dented.

Dempsey had thought of scrapping the car, but time was not with him for that. Anyway, it should make it to Lydd Airport without any problems. Then off to France, and away from all this trouble.

On the motorway, Dempsey was left with his thoughts.

How was Chang alive?

Why had Chalmers set him up?

Who was Chalmers working for?

Was Chang working for Chalmers?

Dempsey had convinced himself that Chang and Chalmers were connected with each other.

Suddenly the radio caught Dempsey's attention. "Police have announced that the elderly tailor found dead in his shop this morning was beaten to death. But a more startling revelation has come after the death of Bernard Cohen, that he may have been a top arms dealer. Police have said the cellar of the shop in London was filled with handguns, rifles, and machine guns...."

Dempsey switched off the radio, tears beginning to well up in his eyes, and sorrow in his heart. In a fit of anger, he slapped the palms of his hands on the steering wheel as tears rolled over his cheeks.

Dempsey wiped his eyes, in his mind the memory of the man who was like a father to him, someone who was there when he needed advice or a shoulder to cry on. The assassin saw a motorway sign that read Lydd, twenty miles. Dempsey knew it would not be long now.

The door collapsed inward from the force of it being kicked in. With the door hanging by one hinge, Robert Chang entered, his 9mm Beretta the length of an arm in front of him.

Chang's eyes darted around the corridor and any door which led off it. As he followed the corridor down, he pushed open every door he passed and glanced inside, wary of anyone who might be there. A bathroom, a bedroom, a kitchen, and a broom cupboard, but no one there. The door at the end of the corridor was open, and Chang approached it very carefully.

He entered what was the living room, and convinced there was no one there, he positioned his gun back in its holster. As he surveyed the room, he noticed a photograph on the other side of the room. A close inspection of the photograph brought a smile to his face. "Mrs. Dempsey, I don't remember you being that pretty."

As Chang walked past the television, his arm brushed the screen, and he felt a small static charge.

"Must have just missed you, John. Now where have you gone? Chang continued to look through drawers, the contents beginning to pile up on the floor. He searched the cabinets in the living room, finding nothing. His lack of patience showed more and more as his search brought him nothing, until he came across a small red diary.

Chang held the small book up to his eyes, noticing that at some time the book had been folded against its cover. Instead of neatly going back together as a nice little book when closed, it stayed open to the page where it was folded.

Chang opened it to the page: Jimmy Flynn, Lydd Airport, and a phone number.

"He's leaving the country, the fucker's getting out of the country," muttered Chang as he put the diary in his pocket.

The Oriental was just about ready to leave when he heard a young man's voice calling. "Mr. Willard, are you alright?"

Chang never answered; instead, he got near to the door entrance and waited.

"Hello, is there anyone there?"

Chang noticed that the voice was getting nearer.

The second the young man's head looked into the living room, Robert Chang hit it. With Chang's fist coming across like a lightning bolt, the youth never even saw the punch as it landed on the side of his head, forcing him to spin around.

The blow, to Chang's surprise, did not knock the young man over. Before the young man could regain his senses, though, Chang grabbed a hold of his head and put him into a kind of headlock. The youth, feeling the growing pressure around his neck, let out a stifled yell.

With one quick, powerful movement, the youth's neck gave out a sickening crack. His body suddenly went limp, and Chang let go. The youth fell in a crumpled mess to the floor. Chang looked at the body and laughed when he saw that the youth could not control his bowels during the fracas. Chang was still laughing when he left.

Chapter Thirteen

At first, Dempsey could not remember where Jimmy Flynn's office—it was just a hut, really—was, but everything soon came back to him. As Dempsey parked the half-wrecked Fiesta, he spotted the man he wanted, his friend, Jimmy Flynn. The assassin got out of his car and walked towards the pilot, carrying the sports holdall that he had brought with him.

"Jimmy!" shouted Dempsey.

"John, what brings you to these parts?" replied Flynn, his soft Irish accent sounding as velvety as a pint of Guinness.

"I left a message on your answer phone. Didn't you get it?"

"Fucking thing doesn't work properly, anyway," said the pilot with a smile. "So what can I do for you?"

"I've got to get out of the country. I was thinking of France," said Dempsey.

"You been a naughty boy again, John?" asked Flynn.

"You could say that."

"When did you want to go?"

"Tonight. Is that possible?" said Dempsey, looking at the Irishman.

"Tonight it is then." Flynn smiled at the hitman. "Cup of tea in the meantime?"

Dempsey had worked with Flynn on two previous occasions, and each time Flynn had helped him to flee the country after a hit. Flynn was thirty-eight, handsome, and well-built. His dodgy activities were known to the police, but like Teflon, they couldn't find anything that would stick. At heart, Flynn was a good man and would try to help anyone who was in a predicament.

Dempsey nodded to the invitation of refreshment and followed the pilot, who had begun to walk towards a portacabin. Inside, it was warm and snug, a marked contrast from outside. Flynn flicked the switch on the kettle and grabbed two mugs.

"Milk and sugar for you, John?" asked the pilot. Dempsey nodded in reply and glanced around the portacabin.

There was a map of the area on the wall, plus what appeared to be some certificates. A shelf which had some files on it was above an untidy desk in the corner.

"Won't be a minute, so it won't," said the Irishman.

Dempsey looked at Flynn, admiring his looks. As far as Dempsey knew, Flynn was older than him, but he only looked about twenty-five.

"I take it this is all hush-hush," said Flynn.

The expression on Dempsey's face gave him the answer.

"We'll leave about seven; it'll be dark by then. To get you to France, John, will cost you five thousand pounds. Aircraft fuel is not cheap, you know."

"I'll send it on to you, if that's okay," replied Dempsey, knowing that's how they did business in the past. The pilot nodded as he poured the water into the mugs and began stirring.

"There's a small airfield just outside Rouen that I usually use. It'll be alright to land there, so it will." Dempsey noticed Flynn looking out at the window. "Well I'm a popular boy today, aren't' I," said Flynn.

Dempsey looked out of the window and saw the Porsche, and he waited to see who got out. When he saw the suit, he knew who it was.

"It's Chang," Dempsey shouted.

"Do you know him?" asked Flynn.

"You could say that. He's killed three people that I loved," said Dempsey as he withdrew the Desert Eagle from its holster. Flynn saw the gun.

"I don't want any trouble, John, nothing like that," said the pilot, pointing at the hand gun. "Look, hide behind the desk, and I'll get rid of him."

"If you don't, I'll kill him."

"Okay, John," said Flynn, his hands telling Dempsey to calm down. The assassin knelt down behind the desk and watched.

Flynn opened the door to his so-called office and approached the Chinaman. "Can I help you in anyway, my friend?" asked the pilot nervously.

"Looking for Jimmy Flynn," said Chang.

"That's me, so it is. How can I help?"

"Do you know a John Dempsey?"

"That I do, haven't seen him for years, though. Why, is there something wrong?" asked Flynn, enjoying the act.

"Not yet, Mr. Flynn. If you see him call me, here's my number," said Chang, handing him a business card. "Good day to you, Mr. Flynn." Chang turned and headed back towards his Porsche.

Flynn climbed the three steps to his portacabin door and opened it.

"There you go, John, no violence. Much easier, isn't it?"

"Mr. Flynn," came the voice. The pilot turned to see Chang standing there pointing a pump-action shotgun at him. "I don't like being lied to, Mr. Flynn."

"Don't know what you mean," said Flynn, his voice nervous.

"The Fiesta, Mr. Flynn. Who do you think put all those holes in it?" said Chang as he smiled.

Chang's smile was the last thing Jimmy Flynn saw. The Remington 870 roared into action, the first shot hitting Flynn in the left shoulder, ripping through until it destroyed the deltoid muscle. Flynn spun around, goblets of blood and flesh flying from the wound.

Chang walked quickly to the entrance of the portacabin, pumping the fore-end stock then firing another shot, this time hitting Flynn full in the face. Flynn's head reacted like an exploding watermelon, depositing pieces of the cranium and the brain all around the inside of the small room.

Dempsey reacted as soon as he could, letting off four shots at the Chinaman, who ducked but was not undeterred. Chang fired another shot from the doorway, this time destroying the files above Dempsey's head. Dempsey returned with three more shots before he had to reload. Again Chang fired the Remington, and a hole appeared in the wall to Dempsey's right.

Dempsey slammed in another clip of the 11.17mm bullets ducking as another blast came from the Remington.

"Come on, John, stick your head out so I can blow it off," shouted the Chinese hitman. Dempsey did not reply; his attention was focused on how to escape from this madman.

When looking around the interior of the portacabin, Dempsey for the first time saw Flynn. Where Flynn's head had been was now a piece of meat which looked ready for the bacon counter at Safeway. Ten feet to Dempsey's left was another door, also leading to the outside. If Dempsey could get through it, he may have time to escape and get away.

There wasn't really any other choice for Dempsey, except for the door. Chang had everything else covered; there was no other way. Dempsey got in a more upright position but stayed on his haunches. With his Desert Eagle pointed and ready to fire, he took a deep breath.

"Chang, you wanker," shouted Dempsey, waiting for a response.

"Come on out, Dempsey, and prepare to die," replied the Chinaman.

"Go fuck yourself," said Dempsey.

Dempsey fingered the trigger of the Desert Eagle, which bucked in is hand as shot after shot came out. At the same time, Dempsey charged at the door. As the seventh and final blast came from Dempsey's gun, he leapt at the door, hoping his weight would be enough to carry him through to the outside.

On impact, the door collapsed, pulling the hinges out along with parts of the frame. Dempsey crashed to the ground, the force of the fall knocking the wind out of him, but he knew he could not stop. As he landed, he heard the explosion of Chang's Remington one more time behind him, the impact causing even more door frame to fly through the air.

Immediately Dempsey got up and began to sprint toward a white Escort about twenty yards away. Chang appeared at the door frame, his Remington aimed at his target. The pull of the trigger though gave no reaction, and Chang furiously pumped the fore-end stock, soon realising he had fired all the cartridges.

Once he got nearer to the Escort, Dempsey saw there was an occupant in the driver's seat. He tugged at the passenger door until it opened.

"Get out of my car," bellowed the pretty redhead.

"Please help me. There's a man trying to kill me," interrupted Dempsey.

"Bullshit," replied the redhead.

Her reply was cut short when she saw the explosion of blood and flesh coming from Dempsey's right shoulder, the bullet exiting through the windscreen. Chang had reverted to his 9mm Beretta and, for the first time, tasted success. Dempsey fell forward into the passenger seat, and the redhead let out a shriek as droplets of blood sprayed her face.

"Now will you drive?" pleaded Dempsey, pained expression on his face.

The redhead looked beyond Dempsey to Chang, who had raised his handgun again. After turning the ignition key, the redhead floored the accelerator. The wheels spun uncontrollably as she sought traction on the wet and muddy grass. Suddenly the car shot off past Chang, who by now was very close. Chang let off one shot, which missed entirely, and his eyes centred on the number plate.

"You can slow down now," muttered Dempsey, touching his newly acquired wound.

"What?" she responded, not really listening at all.

"I said you can slow down now."

"Oh, right," said the redhead, who then glanced at the wound. "Looks like it went right through."

"What, are you a doctor?" asked Dempsey, grimacing as he touched the wound.

"A vet, actually. I was here looking at an injured dog," she replied. "Why did he want to kill you?"

"You don't need to know that. Where do you live? Near here?"

"In Dymchurch, and no, it's not that far."

"Can you treat this wound?" asked Dempsey, realising just how pretty she was.

"You need a hospital, and that's where we're going."

"Hospitals report bullet wounds to the police," stated Dempsey.

"If someone's trying to kill you, then surely the police are who you need."

"It's not as easy as that," responded Dempsey, again catching the driver's good looks.

"Seems pretty easy to me."

"Can you treat this wound?" repeated Dempsey, his voice more determined needing to know now.

"I've patched up bullet wounds on animals...you don't look any different, so I don't see why not," said the redhead. For the first time, she really looked at Dempsey's face and saw the pain he was experiencing. "My house is about six miles away. I'll patch you up there."

"Thank you," replied Dempsey, his attention returned to the road and the wing mirror, but he could not help the odd glance at this pretty woman next to him.

"So what's your name, then?" questioned the driver.

"Dempsey, John Dempsey," answered the hitman, not bothering to give a false name. "And you?"

"Marie Jarvis."

The journey took no more than fifteen minutes.

Chapter Fourteen

Robert Chang had only one clue to the possible whereabouts of John Dempsey, and that was the number plate of the white Escort. The Oriental pulled the red Porsche over to the layby, removed his mobile phone from his inside jacket pocket, and punched in the necessary numbers.

"Hello, DC Short, how can I help you?" came the reply.

"Brian, how are you?" said Chang.

"Who's that? Is that you, Chang?" asked the policeman, still unsure as to who it actually was.

"I thought you would have known my voice by now, Brian."

"What do you want, Chang? I'm busy."

"Just an address, that's all," said Chang, his voice coming across as though he was some kind of creep.

"Look, Chang, I don't have time for this. I'm too busy," stated Brian Short as he lit up yet another cigarette.

"You weren't fucking busy when you wanted that cocaine, was you? Perhaps your inspector would like to hear about your nasal habits," threatened Chang, his voice growing more urgent.

"Okay, okay, tell me what you need to know, and I'll get back to you," conceded the policeman.

"Good, now we know where we are, don't we? The registration number is C422 YTR, a white Escort. Name and address, please, Brian," ordered Chang.

"You know what, Chang? You are the biggest cunt I know. I'll call when I have the information," said Short, slamming the phone down. Chang put his mobile away and chuckled.

Marie Jarvis's house was a small but spacious bungalow with a large garden. When they entered, Dempsey was taken aback by the view from the window.

"Wait here, I'll get my bag, said Marie, who scampered back through the front door to her car. Dempsey removed his leather jacket, for the first time showing the aftermath of the injury. The white T-shirt that Dempsey wore was dripping with blood and sweat.

Marie re-entered the room and saw the full extent of the gun wound—as well as the firearm under Dempsey's left armpit.

"Tell me, when your friend was trying to kill you, did you try and kill him back?" asked Marie, her gaze fixed on the Desert Eagle.

"Yeah, of course I did," replied Dempsey, realising she had seen the handgun.

"You'll have to take that off and the T-shirt."

"I may need some help," said Dempsey, stuttering as he tried to remove the shoulder holster. With a great deal of trouble, Dempsey pulled the holster over his shoulders, grimacing at the pain that was coming from the wound. Marie could see from his face that removing his shirt was becoming quite an ordeal.

"Hang on, this might be easier," remarked the vet as she removed a pair of surgical scissors from her bag. She proceeded to cut the shirt from Dempsey's body, a small grimace appearing on her face when she saw the wound.

"You're lucky it went right through," said Marie.

"How come I don't feel very lucky?" retorted Dempsey looking at the redhead in front of him.

"Wait here, I'll get some hot water so we can clean you up," stated the vet, who then wandered off to the kitchen.

Within a minute she returned with a bowl of hot water and a flannel, and began to clean the wound up.

"Why are you helping me?" asked Dempsey, stammering as she wiped away some of the congealed blood.

"I don't know...you seem like you need it," she replied as she fished in her bag for some bandages.

Detective Inspector Grant was becoming a desperate man. So far, he still had little to go on. The photofit picture had not yielded anything except some hoax calls, and the pressure was mounting on him for a result. Grant looked up as, preceded by a knock, his office door was opened. It was Miller.

"What is it, Graham?" asked Grant, sounding impatient and as though he did not want to be disturbed.

"You're not gonna believe this, Guv...that old tailor who got killed in London this morning, fingerprints found there cross-match with our Mr. Bob Johnson. They reckon the cellar was full of guns, a miniature arsenal. A top quality sniper's rifle was found near the body in an attache case. SOCO are checking that out first. If Johnson's our man, that is where he was probably supplied with the gun."

"Good stuff, Graham."

"That's not all though, Guv. The body of a youth was found in a flat in west London and guess what. The same fingerprints are all over the flat. It belongs to a Steve Willard."

"You checked him out?"

"Nothing on him at all, Guv."

"Shit, still now we're getting somewhere. Contact the officers in charge of both cases and explain the situation. Tell them we want every last detail. I'll phone DCI Collins and tell him to cross-match the prints from the pub, and with a bit of luck they'll be the same. Our friend Johnson, Corbett, Willard, or whatever he fucking calls himself is in deep shit," said Grant, smiling.

Marie Jarvis had made a good job of the wound in Dempsey's shoulder, treating it and then bandaging it. As Dempsey rested on her settee she made some tea, returning with the teapot on a tray with some mugs and a small jug of milk.

"Do you live here on your own?" inquired the wounded assassin.

"I have since I divorced my husband. Part of the settlement. Are you married?" asked Marie.

"Was. She died three years ago, with my daughter," replied Dempsey, the tone of his voice changing.

"I'm sorry to hear that," said the vet, realising she had touched a raw nerve. "Do you miss them?"

"There isn't a day when I don't think of them."

Marie could see the hurt on Dempsey's face, but this had nothing to do with the bullet wound in his shoulder; this was deeper, much deeper inside, somewhere that could not be treated by medicine.

"Do you take sugar?" asked Marie, trying to change the subject.

"Yes, two please," responded Dempsey, who wiped his eyes with the fingers of his left hand.

The vet handed Dempsey the mug of tea and looked at him, feeling sorry for him but finding him attractive at the same time.

"You need rest, and you'll be safe here until I come back from the shops. I'm not expecting anyone, so you won't be disturbed," explained Marie.

"Thanks, thanks for everything," said Dempsey.

With that Marie left, and Dempsey leaned back into the sofa and closed his eyes. Soon he was asleep.

Chapter Fifteen

Marie Jarvis returned about an hour later, her entrance not waking Dempsey, who was sleeping heavily after taking some painkillers. Spaghetti bolognese being one of her specialty dishes, Marie set about making it with the ingredients she had bought.

While letting it cook, she returned to where Dempsey slept, and sat in the armchair opposite, admiring his muscular body. Suddenly Dempsey woke up yelling, but he stopped when he realised what he was doing.

Startled, Marie rushed over to him, noticing the sweat that was coming from his body.

"What is it? Are you alright?" she wanted to know.

"A nightmare, the same fucking nightmare of when they died," mumbled Dempsey.

"Who? Your wife and daughter?"

"Yes. They were murdered, and I could have stopped it," said Dempsey. Marie looked on, wanting to know more. "Three years ago I was assigned to do a job," began Dempsey.

"Assigned, what do you mean assigned?" interrupted the vet.

"I work for the government. I do special jobs for them," stated Dempsey.

Marie immediately understood what he meant: the weapon he carried...shoot-out at the airport...it all came together now. The realisation of it all shocked Marie, and she returned to her chair, feeling a kind of wariness about the man opposite.

"I was assigned to kill a man whom I admired, a man who had been my commanding officer in the army, a man who had motivated and helped me. If it wasn't for him, I'd be nothing. At first I didn't want to do it, but realised I had to. After I had carried out the assignment, I returned home to find my wife and daughter being held by a gunman," said Dempsey.

Marie's eyes lit up when he mentioned they had been held.

"I told him the job had been done and he should let them go, but he would have none of it, saying he had to have a phone call, he needed confirmation. Suddenly Lisa, my daughter, was running at me, and he shot her in the back of the head. Then he shot my wife and killed her as well. In a moment of anger, I opened fire, and until today I thought I had killed that bastard." Tears welled in Dempsey's eyes as he remembered that night three years ago.

Marie sat next to him and embraced him, feeling the pain he was going through. As she looked up to him, their eyes locked together. Marie kissed Dempsey and he responded, their tongues touching and probing each other's mouths.

The hitman maneuvered his hand over her T-shirt, massaging her breast. His hand then found its way inside her loose-fitting top, his hand stroking her tummy until reaching the smooth skin of her breast, which he kneaded until he felt the nipple scraping at his palm. Still their lips were locked together, their tongues darting from their mouths. Marie's hand lowered to Dempsey's groin and began to rub, feeling the stiffness which emerged underneath. As they continued to embrace, Dempsey winced, his shoulder causing him pain. His hand, though, continued to probe her warm body.

Marie broke the kiss and took Dempsey's hand, leading him to the bedroom. There, they made love.

Chapter Sixteen

Dempsey awoke the next morning wondering where he was; then it all came back to him. He looked to his side to find an empty bed, then proceeded to put on his jeans. As he walked from the bedroom, he found what he sought—Marie Jarvis.

"Good morning," said Marie, smiling. "Sleep well?"

"Very well, thank you," responded Dempsey, his own smile spreading across his own face.

"Tea?" asked Marie, holding up her own mug of liquid refreshment.

"Yes, please."

The pretty redhead jumped up from her chair and headed for the kitchen. Dempsey's eyes followed her as she walked, her long T-shirt coming just above her knees, her body looking as beautiful as anything he had ever seen. Dempsey stretched his injured shoulder, and although it felt tight, he could manage with it.

As Dempsey sat in the armchair, Marie returned with a mug of steaming tea, which Dempsey accepted. Marie sat in the chair opposite and looked at Dempsey.

"What are you going go do?" inquired Marie. Dempsey looked at her as he sipped the hot tea.

"I don't know yet. I can't give myself up to the police. Probably going to France is still my best shot," responded Dempsey.

"What about this Chalmers fellow, what if you tackle him?"

"He'd only deny it was anything to do with him. I'm practically on my own with this one."

Marie got up and approached the assassin. "You're not on your own now," she said as she knelt in front of him and kissed his hand.

Dempsey looked at her and smiled. For the first time in three years he felt happy.

"I think you should see more of sunny Dymchurch," said Marie. "The fresh air will do you good, it'll help you to think. Come out for a walk with me today."

"What if I'm spotted by the police?"

"You can't stay inside forever."

"Okay, I'll come with you for a walk," replied Dempsey. Marie smiled at Dempsey, with their eyes locked together they joined at the mouth, feeling each others probing tongues.

Marie broke the kiss. "I'd better change the dressing, hadn't I?" Dempsey looked at her and smiled; memories of his wife and daughter had suddenly disappeared.

DIP Peter Grant sat at the large table, awaiting the entry of Detective Chief Inspector Collins. Opposite was DI Tom Rogers, and to the left, DI John Bush. Grant knew Bush from training at Hendon, a good copper by all accounts and looking for promotion. Rogers, though, was known only by reputation: Four years in the drug squad had put ten years on his age. Each one of them was an inspector looking for the "big case" to give them elevation to a higher rank, and each one currently believed he had that case.

Detective Chief Inspector Sean Collins entered the room, and the three lower ranked officers stood as a sign of recognition.

"Please, gentlemen, sit down. My apologies for keeping you waiting," stated Collins, his Yorkshire accent broad as he spoke. All four men sat at the same time.

"Gentlemen, I have asked you here because we appear to have a common factor in the cases we're all currently involved with," said Collins, his eyes glancing from one inspector to another. "It appears the same set of fingerprints have been found in each case; therefore, I feel we should put all our evidence together to try and find this man. I think you all know each other so there's no need for introductions. Let's get down to it."

The chief inspector's eyes met with Bush's. "John, what have you got?" asked the DCI, his voice sounding like the archetypal cricket commentator.

"Well sir, we were called in when the body of an elderly tailor, Bernard Cohen, was found beaten to death. The fingerprints that you mentioned were found all over the premises, including downstairs, where we found an extraordinary amount of firearms, grenades, rifles, and a lot of other hardware," stated Bush, his explanation clear and rehearsed, as though he were in court.

"When the body was discovered by an elderly lady, there was this man standing over him. When she went running out of the shop, this guy followed and was fired upon by an Asian man.

"The gunfight that ensued was, according to witnesses, 'like something from a movie.' Sadly the old woman was shot in the crossfire and the two suspects ended up having a car chase through London."

"What about descriptions, John, anything there?" asked Collins, who was writing every detail down in shorthand.

"The fellow in the tailor's had black hair, about six feet tall or so, well-built, and knew what he was doing with the gun."

"Sound's like our man," interrupted Grant.

"Hang on a moment, Peter. You'll get your chance," said Collins as though he was reprimanding a six-year-old at a junior school. "Carry on, John."

"The Chinaman was described as six-feet-two, dark hair, and well-dressed. He, too, was no apparent stranger to firearms."

"This Chinaman, could he have killed the tailor, or is it almost certain it was the other chap?" inquired the DCI.

"Nothing is certain, sir. Many fingerprints were found, some we don't know," answered Bush.

"Thanks, John. Now, Peter, what have you got to say?" asked Collins, his steely blue eyes focused on the Kentish policeman.

"We believe our man was staying in a bed and breakfast, using that as his base whilst waiting for the chance to kill his intended victim. We also think he is the same man who was involved in a fight in a pub, where he was described as fighting as if he was a professional. In that I don't mean as a boxer but as a man trained to fight, as in, say, the armed forces." Grant broke off momentarily to take in some liquid; there was a jug of water on the table and he helped himself.

When he was ready he continued, "We had many descriptions of the man, all of them describing a dark-haired, six-foot tall, well-built man. One of those description was from a young PC who spoke at length to the suspect the morning after the fight in the pub. We also have the fingerprints in his room and at the pub." Grant again guzzled at the water.

"The PC who spoke to him, was this an interview?" questioned Collins.

"No, sir, apparently a word of warning. The two men who were beaten up refused to press charges. The PC was telling him merely to be careful of possible repercussions," replied Grant, returning the glass to the table.

"Any names for this suspect, Peter?" queried Collins.

"Went by the name of Bob Johnson," answered Grant.

The DCI finished writing his notes and brought his attention to Detective Inspector Tom Rogers, who had sat there quite patiently while the others spoke.

"Tom, how about you?" said Collins.

"The body of a youth was found in a flat. The door had been kicked in and the place appeared as though it had been searched. The victim suffered from a broken neck," relayed Rogers as he checked with his notebook. "The flat was in the name of Steven Willard. Neighbours say he was away a lot, but very quiet when he was there. We found prints all over the flat, one we think is Willard's, which are the same as the ones

Peter and John have. A second set was cross-checked and matched a set picked up at the tailor's shop."

"Why didn't you fucking tell us?" demanded Bush, unaware of this evidence.

"Why didn't you check it, John?" replied Rogers with his voice raised.

"Come on gentlemen, that's enough!" shouted Collins, his face reddening from the outburst. "John, you should have checked it, now shut up. What description is there of this Willard, then, Tom?"

"Much the same as the others—dark hair, six feet, and well-built," responded Rogers, still annoyed by Bush's outburst.

"Any photographs at the flat we can use?" asked Collins.

"Only of a woman and a young girl, possibly her daughter. There was an address stamped on the back of a photographers studio. My sergeant is checking that out now," finished Rogers, giving a "fuck you" look to Bush.

Collins had heard the others speak and was now ready to put his evidence on the table. He put his notepad down and began to speak in a broad Yorkshire dialect. "After some investigating, we, too, came up with much the same as you chaps. The prints and the description are identical, so I think we can safely say without doubt that this chap—Willard, Johnson, Corbett, or whatever he calls himself—is definitely our man. What connection this Chinaman has, I really don't know. Maybe that second set of prints are his.

"General feeling is that this Willard chap is a professional...working for who, I don't know. If the Chinaman's involved, it could be triads or possibly another gang thing. Possible armed forces was mentioned. Have you checked military records, Peter?" asked Collins.

"They're being looked at now, sir," came the reply from Grant.

"John, the firearms that were found at the tailors, could any of them have been used at the shootings?" questioned the DCI.

"Forensics are still going through the arsenal of weapons. A rifle was found near the body, and there is a possibility we may find a murder weapon there," said Bush.

In general the four policemen had nothing to go on, except a set of fingerprints and a description. Collins looked disappointed; his intentions had been to come away from this meeting with a positive attitude, not to be where they were when they first entered the room.

"Well, gentlemen," began the Detective Chief Inspector, "we can only continue as we have and hopefully a breakthrough will appear." Collins' disappointment was obvious to the men in the room. "Thank you all for attending, good day."

Collins got up from the chair and left quickly, leaving the other three still in the room. Bush was still angry at Rogers and intended to tell him what he thought of him.

"If you ever do that again, Rogers, I'll make sure you get fucked up," snarled the angry inspector, his Cockney accent coming over very strongly.

"Don't threaten me, you pathetic shit. If you had done your job properly, there wouldn't be any worries, would there?" bellowed Rogers.

Bush would have no more of it and lunged at his fellow inspector, throwing a right hand at him and catching him square on the jaw. Rogers fell in a heap on the floor, almost unconscious. Grant grabbed Bush, who was about to follow up.

"Alright John, calm down, will you," said Grant, who was now pulling Bush back. Rogers began to get up, rubbing his bruised jaw.

"I'll fucking have you for this, Bush! They'll throw you out of the force for this," threatened Rogers, who made his way to the door and left.

"Feel better now, John?" asked Grant with a hint of irony in his voice.

"Fucking wanker," responded the inspector, who also decided it was time to leave.

Grant stood in the room alone and shook his head. Here we are, he thought, all on the same side but fighting each other. With that, he left.

Dempsey wasn't too sure whether going out was a good idea or not. Wanted all over the country by the police, and here he was, out for a leisurely stroll on the beach.

"Must be nice in the summer," said Dempsey, his gaze falling to Marie, who was holding on to his arm as they walked.

"The beach gets quite full. Many come here for their holidays or days at the seaside," said Marie, her nose red from the cold weather. Dempsey noticed it and suggested they go for a cup of tea somewhere. Marie suggested a small cafe not far away, and they headed for it.

The walk to the cafe lasted about five minutes. On entering, they immediately felt the warmth of the place. Only two unoccupied tables were left—one at the window and another towards the rear near the counter. Dempsey elected for the one nearer the counter; after all, he might be recognised near the window.

Before sitting down, Marie removed her coat and hung it on the back of her chair. Dempsey would have done the same except for his gun in its holster and the fact that it would be too painful to take his jacket off, anyway. After they sat down, a small, frail lady wearing a pink apron approached their table.

"What will it be then, my loves?" asked the woman as though she had known them all her life.

"A tea for me, and a doughnut, please," requested Marie, whose red nose had now turned to its normal colour.

"Just a tea for me, thank you," said Dempsey. "I'm cutting down." Marie laughed at the remark.

"Won't be two ticks," said the lady, who had begun to scurry off to behind the counter.

"Any thoughts on what you are going to do?" asked Marie, looking at the assassin.

"Not really, I'll probably go back to London and confront Chalmers...see what he has to say for himself," replied Dempsey.

Deep down though, Dempsey wanted to stay in Dymchurch with Marie. Who knows, settle down and start a new life? Marie also felt the same but decided not to push it. Within two minutes, they had their tea in front of them.

Robert Chang had decided his battered Porsche was maybe a bit too conspicuous, so he elected for a trip to Avis and hired a car from there. He now had the address of Marie's bungalow and was heading there with the aid of a road map. Before leaving in the hired care, he had transferred the shotgun and cartridges, and was ready for Dempsey in every way.

Chang stopped at some traffic lights and observed the people who were crossing. His eyes fixed on a pretty blonde whose backside moved rhythmically as she walked, and his eyes followed her as she passed him on the other side of the street. Perverted thoughts were going through his head when he looked inside a nearby cafe. It couldn't be—John Dempsey sitting there with a cup of tea in his hand.

Chang spotted the lights were now green and drove until he found a place to turn around. A small drive, on the left, leading to an engineers, would be the ideal place. Chang used the drive to turn around and headed back for the small cafe.

The Chinaman stopped the car just before the cafe and got out. Before he opened the boot, he looked around to check if anyone was near, and when satisfied, he opened the boot and pumped five cartridges that the Remington 870 required, then put a handful in his pocket.

Chang slammed the boot down and headed for the cafe door, taking in deep breaths as he walked, his eyes still everywhere watching for anyone or anything. Before opening the door, he pumped the shotgun so it was ready to fire.

Just at the second Chang opened the door, Dempsey looked up and spotted him.

"Jesus! It's Chang, get down!" shouted Dempsey. Marie dived for the floor as the first blast from the Remington came. The table erupted in front of them as Dempsey hit the floor, going for his own gun.

The other people in the cafe began to shout and scream as Chang again pumped the beast that was in his hands. With people trying to scurry from the cafe, Dempsey could not risk a shot so turned his attention to Marie who was cowering against the counter.

"Marie, go out the back, I'll follow," said Dempsey.

As she began to move, another shot come, this time above Dempsey's head, causing pieces of plaster to fall upon him. A have-a-go hero had now tackled Chang, and Dempsey saw this as a chance to escape. The hero, though, was soon cut down to size. Chang used the butt of his gun to crush the man's nose, and it exploded on impact. Chang spotted Dempsey moving towards the back entrance and started to move quickly after him.

Dempsey followed Marie through the back door and considered his limited options.

"Keep going Marie. I'll catch up with you," said Dempsey. Marie looked at him and then turned, scampering down the alley, avoiding rubbish.

Dempsey returned the Desert Eagle to its holster and picked up a piece of wood from the broken pallet on the ground. He then stood just behind the door, waiting for Chang to appear. He didn't have to wait long, as Chang sprung through the door.

Dempsey swung the piece of wood like a baseball player going for the home run. The wood hit Chang in the chest, causing him to drop the pump action shotgun. Chang reeled from the strike, but this was just the beginning. With his head bent forward, Dempsey unleashed a kick which struck Chang accurately in the face. The force of the kick broke the Chinaman's nose.

Again Dempsey moved towards his prey. Chang stood there, dazed and confused, blood flowing through his hands, which were covering his face. Another kick (this time at Chang's genitals) hit home, finally bringing Chang to his knees.

Chang had nothing to come back with, but still Dempsey had not finished. He withdrew the Desert Eagle from under his arm and pointed the gun at Chang, who had begun to recover slightly. Chang looked at Dempsey and smiled.

"All a big laugh to you, isn't it, Chang? Well laugh at this, you fucking cunt."

Dempsey raised the gun and fired. The shot was aimed at Chang's left arm and hit just above the elbow, causing an explosion of blood. Chang shouted in agony, the pain from his nose and genitals all but forgotten.

"Still laughing, are we?" yelled Dempsey. The sound of sirens approaching could be heard in the distance. Again Dempsey raised the handgun and fired, this time a fountain of blood flowed from Chang's right arm. Chang screamed in pain, agony excruciating.

Now lying in a pool of blood, Chang was helpless. He couldn't move his arms and knew death was around the corner. Dempsey raised the gun one more time, and the sirens got nearer and nearer.

"Why did Chalmers set me up?" asked Dempsey, the gun pointing at Chang's head.

"Go get fucked," spat Chang, blood from his nose had flowed over his mouth and some hit Dempsey in the face. Dempsey stooped over Chang and dragged him up. With the Desert Eagle now positioned under his chin, Chang had no escape.

"For the last time, why did Chalmers set me up?" repeated Dempsey.

"I said get fucked," responded Chang.

"Then fuck you and die," said Dempsey. His finger touched the trigger, and the Desert Eagle exploded into action. The 11.17mm bullet exited from the top of Chang's head, spreading pieces of red and grey matter all over the wall. The Chinaman slumped to the ground.

The sound of the sirens brought Dempsey back to his senses, and he looked at the dead man on the ground. The assassin's shoulder was aching and felt warm. It was only after he felt the wound that he realised he had blood on his hand, his blood. The gunshot wound had been stretched to its limit and had finally given out. Blood flowed freely from his shoulder. Dempsey began to run down the alley, not knowing where he was going. Soon he saw the main road and slowed down so as not to bring attention to himself. As he entered the main road he looked back up the street and saw nothing but police cars. Then he heard Marie's voice, calling him from the other side of the road in her Escort.

Dempsey walked over to the car and got inside. Marie put her foot on the accelerator and pulled away.

"Is he dead?" asked Marie, her voice trembling.

"Yes, he's dead," replied Dempsey.

The journey back to Marie's house was a silent one.

Chapter Seventeen

It took Peter Grant about an hour to return to his police station in Kent. On the way, he could think of nothing except the Lomax murder. He needed a breakthrough but was not sure if he was going to get one.

After entering his office he was met by his sergeant, Graham Miller.

"Graham, any luck with those military records yet?" asked Grant, who had now sat down and was massaging the bridge of his nose.

"No, Guv, not a thing. But something else has come up," answered the detective sergeant. Grant looked up from his desk, eager to hear the new information.

"Two men have been found dead—one at Lydd Airport and one in Dymchurch."

"So what has that to do with us?" questioned Grant, obviously disappointed with the information, as his remark was abrupt and almost rude.

"The body found at Lydd Airport had most of his head spread over the insides of a portacabin, the victim of a shotgun. The one in Dymchurch apparently opened fire with a shotgun in a small cafe. He was found out the back with the top of his head missing, also caused by a gun," finished Miller.

"Jesus Christ! People are suddenly having a bad habit of dying from gunshot wounds. Do we have names for these victims?" enquired Grant, who suddenly was now very interested.

"Jimmy Flynn and Robert Chang," replied Miller, referring to a piece of paper that he had in his hand.

"Chang!" emphasised Grant.

"Chinese, apparently. Well-dressed and well-off by the looks of things."

"DI John Bush mentioned a Chinaman. Had a shoot-out at the scene of the Cohen murder with another bloke. Get in touch with whoever is in charge down there, tell them to fax his fingerprints to Detective Inspector

John Bush. I'll phone John and let him know. Then I'll get in touch with Collins. This could be the breakthrough we're looking for Graham," stated Grant, who was now enthusiastic again.

Miller rushed off to carry out his orders, while Grant picked up the telephone. He quickly punched in the numbers he required, and waited for the reply.

"Detective Inspector John Bush speaking. How may I help you?" came the answer.

"John, it's Peter Grant. We've got two dead bodies down in Kent, and one of them is a Chinaman. I'm having the prints faxed to you...hopefully we'll get a match," said Grant with an excited voice.

"Thanks for telling me, Peter. That's more than that wanker Rogers done."

"No problem, John. I'm going to phone Collins and let him know as well," declared Grant.

"Okay, I'll let you know what we get. Talk to you soon," said Bush, hanging up the receiver. As soon as Grant heard the click, he took out Collins' card from his wallet and punched in the numbers, and Collins answered almost immediately. Grant relayed the new information to him; both men were now certain that the breakthrough had finally come.

On returning to Marie's house, Dempsey had finally made a decision. He would return to London and confront Chalmers, find out why he had been set up, and then get out of the country, hopefully with Marie.

Marie was shaken by the affair at the cafe; after all, she had never been shot at before. As soon as they entered the bungalow, Dempsey made some tea, hoping it would calm down Marie.

"I've decided to return to London, Marie. I've got to see Chalmers and find out what's going on."

"Could that not be dangerous? Look at what's happened today," said Marie, trying to change Dempsey's mind.

"If Chalmers is behind this, he would have sent only one man."

"What if it's not Chalmers?" asked Marie, her voice trembling.

"That's a risk I'm going to have to take. Going to London is the only way I can sort this out," said Dempsey.

"What about after, what then?" questioned Marie.

"We could go to France, start a new life. Marie, I want to be with you. Will you come with me?" asked Dempsey.

Marie put the mug of tea on the coffee table and approached Dempsey. They embraced, Marie nestling her head in his chest.

"Yes, John, I'll come to France with you," said Marie as she looked at the assassin. Dempsey looked at the pretty vet, then kissed her. She responded opening her mouth and feeling his probing tongue.

After cross-checking the fingerprints of Robert Chang, Bush did, indeed, make a match from Bernard Cohen's shop. Although they matched, it didn't necessarily prove that he was the killer of the Jewish tailor. But he did feel as though some ground had been broken and contacted DCI Collins. Collins immediately called for the four policemen to get together again, the second time in twenty-four hours.

Peter Grant got the call while he was on his way home. After contacting his wife, he again headed for London. At midnight the roads were not too busy; therefore, the journey did not take as long as earlier in the day. Grant was sure this was the breakthrough they had been looking for, but for some reason he just did not trust DCI Collins. Collins was a control freak, taking charge so he could grab the glory. Grant wasn't going to let him do it this time, though.

The Kentish policeman was back at New Scotland Yard within thirty minutes from leaving for home. He parked his car in the car park and headed for the meeting room they had used earlier, passing through stringent security checks on the way.

On reaching the room, Grant politely knocked on the door before entering. The other three detectives were already in the room talking amongst themselves.

"Come in, Peter, sit down," ordered Collins.

"Thank you, sir," replied Grant as he acknowledged the other two in the room noticing the huge bruise on Tom Roger's chin.

"Now then gentlemen," began Collins, his broad Yorkshire accent seeming to bounce off the walls, "since earlier we have indeed had a development. Two men have been found in Kent, dead. Both from gunshot wounds. One of them was a pilot, Jimmy Flynn, renowned for illegal journeys across the channel and beyond. The other an Oriental, Robert Chang. Fingerprints match a set found in the tailors and this guy Willard's place.

"There is also a match, I've just been informed, at Flynn's so-called office at Lydd airport," said Collins, his eyes searching the other three men for possible ideas. Grant was the first to speak.

"We've all agreed that this guy—Willard, Johnson, and Corbett—are all the same man, yeah?" exclaimed the detective, waiting for agreement from the others, which they all did by nodding their heads. "What if Willard, or whatever you want to call him, had been hired to kill Webster and this guy Chang had also been hired to kill Willard so there is no come back? That would explain their gunfight and car chase here in London," said Grant. The other three were looking at him as if he was grasping at straws.

"Where does this bloke Flynn fit in then?" asked Rogers, sounding as skeptical as ever.

"Flynn was a pilot...maybe he was going to fly Willard out to France or anywhere, and our Chinese friend caught up with him down at Lydd after going through Willard's flat. Someone maybe interrupted him while he was searching Willard's flat and then he killed them," explained Grant.

"A bit thin, ain't it, Peter?" remarked Rogers with a sarcastic laugh.

"So what's your fucking scenario then, Tom?" sneered Grant.

Collins recognised some animosity between them and quickly got involved with the situation. "Okay then Peter, say you're right—the Chinaman killed the tailor, the youth, and Flynn. Who killed the Chinaman? Willard."

"Has to be. The Chinaman pursued Willard from London to the south coast. He wanted Willard dead, there's no doubt of that," answered Grant.

"What do you think, John?" said Collins, asking Bush who had not said a word since the meeting had began.

"I think Peter might have hit it on the head. The Chinaman's fingerprints are everywhere. It was definitely him who walked into the cafe blasting a shotgun. And he was seemingly intent on hurting somebody. A witness said he chased a man and a woman through the back of the cafe, probably Willard and someone who is helping him," stated Bush.

"Tom, anything better?" asked Collins.

"No, nothing. Peter could be right," replied Rogers.

Collins looked at the three men and began to speak. "If the Chinaman's weapon did kill Flynn, we'll soon know because it's being tested now by forensics. We should now hone in on this guy Willard. Catch him and this is all sewn up." Collins looked at Grant and continued, "Peter, you're still involved because of Lomax. Tom and John, tie up any loose ends with the cases you're on. With the Chinaman dead, it would appear that your cases are solved."

Rogers and Bush glanced at each other, waiting for the other to say something. Neither did, so Bush got to his feet and said his goodbyes. As he left, Rogers followed—saying nothing, but giving Grant a rather dirty look. The Kentish policeman replied with an exaggerated smile.

As the door shut Grant also got to his feet and was ready to go when he was stopped by Collins.

"Peter, hang on, will you?"

"Certainly, sir," responded Grant as he returned to his chair.

"If you're right with your theory about the Chinaman, you would have played a blinder. Your name will be mentioned in my report, commending you for your input on this case. If you can catch this Willard chap, you'll be looking at promotion, so don't slouch. I'm relying on you, okay?" stated the senior officer.

"Yes, sir, you can count on me," replied Grant.

"Good. Goodnight to you then, Peter."

Grant nodded and left the room, and his enthusiasm now knew no bounds. Catch Willard, and he would be moving up in the world.

Dempsey had stayed at Marie's bungalow until early morning, and then made his way to London to speak to Chalmers. The farewell was a tearful one. Imagining that Dempsey would not return, Marie begged him not to go and that they could head for France now if he wanted. The hitman said he had to find out what was going on, and promised that he would return. Reluctantly Marie agreed.

Driving along the motorway gave Dempsey time to think about why he had been set up. Was it Chalmers' way of getting him out, or did the order come from higher up, maybe someone in the government, maybe the prime minister himself? Dempsey found that he could not eliminate anyone from the problem.

Dempsey had borrowed Marie's car for the journey. Looking at the speedometer, he realised he was doing eighty-miles-per-hour and immediately slowed to a safer fifty-five in the middle lane.

Dempsey's attention was attracted by the small bullet hole in the windscreen, and it reminded him of Marie and how, if she hadn't let him in the car, Chang would have killed him. The thought of Marie brought a smile to his face and a feeling of contentment inside him.

The journey to London would not take long, but long enough for Dempsey to make his plans for Chalmers. What would he do when he found Chalmers—kill him, hurt him, threaten him, or maybe all three? At this time, Dempsey himself did not know.

Chapter Eighteen

Leonard Chalmers gave progress reports to Peter Campbell almost every day. Today, though, he was the bringer of bad tidings. He would have to tell the home secretary that Dempsey was still alive, and that Chang was dead, probably killed by Demspey. At first, he was going to use the telephone but decided that would make him look weak; after all, Campbell had offered him a job, so being strong was the best policy.

The meeting had been arranged for ten o'clock at Campbell's office. Although Chalmers had been there already several times, he somehow always felt nervous, and today he felt even worse than usual.

As usual Peter Campbell's secretary showed Chalmers into the office. Campbell was behind his desk, this time going through the newspapers.

"Leonard, good to see you, how are you?" enquired the Campbell.

"Very well, thank you, home secretary," responded Chalmers, hesitantly.

"Sit down, Leonard. Now, what news have you brought me?" asked the minister as he folded the newspaper and returned it to the pile upon his desk. Chalmers had not been looking forward to that question, and had wondered whether to lie.

"Well sir, it's Dempsey," stammered Chalmers.

"Finally got rid of him, have we?"

"No. He's still alive," said Chalmers, reluctantly.

"Then you had better get on to your Chinese friend and tell him to pull his finger out," said Campbell, his attention now fully attracted.

"That might not be that easy, sir...you see Chang is dead. Probably killed by Dempsey," stated Chalmers.

"I thought this man Chang was the best. If he was, how can he be dead?"

"Apparently, he was found with bullet wounds down in Kent. As far as I know, he pursued Dempsey down to Dymchurch. Dempsey must have been too quick for him," answered Chalmers.

"Look, Leonard," began Campbell, his voice deadly serious, "Dempsey cannot survive. Make sure he is eliminated from the equation. Within the next two days, I am going to call a press conference which will expose the prime minister for what he really is. There must be no possibility of Dempsey rocking the boat."

Chalmers nodded in agreement. He looked at Campbell and could see a look in his eyes that he had never seen. The home secretary looked worried about his plans.

Campbell again began to talk. "Now, Leonard, if you get rid of Dempsey, there will—as I have said before—be opportunities open to you when I become prime minister." That look in Campbell's eyes had now disappeared as he appeared to be back in his usual mode. "For instance, the man in charge of MI-5 just doesn't cut the ice for me, where as you, Leonard, I think would."

Chalmers again nodded; the thought of running a department like that excited him.

"Okay, sir. Chang may not have been as good as I thought, but rest assured, Dempsey will not be a problem."

"That's good to hear. Leonard, I'm depending on you," said Campbell as he stood and offered his hand to Chalmers. Chalmers shook the hand, the hand that he hoped would give him the job of being in charge of a very important department.

Marie Jarvis had sat in the armchair since Dempsey left earlier that morning. Alone with her thoughts, she had been crying, worried that Dempsey would not return and that they would not escape to France. She had been imagining all kinds of things—Dempsey getting caught, getting shot again, or even getting killed in a motorway pile up.

Her thoughts were soon extinguished by the ring of the front doorbell. Marie looked at the cuckoo clock that was above the fire place. It read ten-thirty, but she wasn't expecting anyone or anything.

This time the door let out a huge knock, as though someone was ready to break it down. What if they were here for Dempsey, trying to kill him again? She quickly ran over to the front window and peeked out. What she saw was a relief to her. A police car.

Marie immediately sprinted to the front door, and the thought of security rocketed through her mind. On opening the door, though, she was soon brought back to earth.

"Mrs. Jarvis," said the man in front of her, "My name's Detective Sergeant Graham Miller." The policeman held up his warrant card so she could see it fully. "I wonder if we could possibly ask you some questions."

"About what, exactly?" said the redhead defensively.

"Could we come in and discuss this, madam?" asked Miller.

Marie nodded and ushered in the Detective Sergeant and WPC. Although Marie never saw them, the curtains at number twenty-four twitched as they had done for the last two days.

When they were inside, Marie offered the two officers a seat which they both took.

"Now, Mrs. Jarvis, is Mr. Jarvis here at all?" began Miller.

"We're divorced, have been for some months now," she replied.

"Any boyfriends, then?" continued Miller.

"What has that got to do with anything?" snapped Marie.

"Well, Mrs. Jarvis, a man fitting one of our descriptions was seen yesterday with you."

"I don't know what you mean, I really don't," lied Marie.

"We think you do, Mrs. Jarvis, so we would like you to accompany us to the police station for further questioning. If you would like to get your coat, we'll be on our way," requested Miller.

Marie sat there, stunned at first, but coming around as to what was happening.

"Please, Mrs. Jarvis, if we can," said Miller, hurrying her.

Marie got up from the armchair and got her coat from the coat stand. She turned around to see the two officers already waiting at the door, and a sudden fear came over her. She had never been in a police station, let alone arrested. The detective sergeant again asked her to hurry herself. In thirty minutes she would be questioned at the police station.

Dempsey had arrived in London at around eleven, fully intent on what he was to do. The journey from Dymchurch had given him time to straighten out his mind and look at things more rationally.

He decided that he would wait for Chalmers to leave his office and then apprehend him, making Chalmers take him to his house. The wait would be a long one.

Peter Grant had raced down to New Romney CID after he had been telephoned by Graham Miller earlier in the morning. Miller had followed up, of his own accord, after hearing about the sighting in Dymchurch.

On arriving at the police station, Grant was met by his sergeant at the front desk. Impatient to know what was going on he began questioning Miller.

"What has she said, Graham, anything?" asked the senior officer as they ascended the stairs.

"Nothing yet, Guv. She's staying quiet," replied the sergeant.

"Where did the sighting come from?"

"A neighbour, been watching the news, saw the photofit, looked out the window and there he was on the opposite side of the road, getting into Marie Jarvis' car," explained Miller.

Grant had followed his sergeant to an interview room on the second floor. Above the door a sign read do not enter when red light is on. Grant again enquired Marie's name. Miller told him and said she had no previous convictions. Then they entered.

Inside, Marie sat behind a desk, looking worried and perplexed. To her right was a woman police constable. Grant and Miller entered the room and sat down opposite the pretty animal doctor.

"Mrs. Jarvis, my name is Peter Grant, Detective Inspector Peter Grant. I'm heading a murder inquiry which you may be able to help us with," stated Grant, looking at the redhead and noticing how attractive she was.

Marie continued to sit there without saying a word.

"A man was seen this morning leaving your bungalow. Could you tell us who that was, please?"

"I don't know what you mean, Inspector," answered Marie.

"Are you saying that a man did not leave your home this morning?" interrupted Miller.

"I'm saying I don't know what you're talking about, or why I am here," declared Marie, who was becoming more confident.

"Mrs. Jarvis, at present you are not under arrest, but that can be changed. I urge you to be cooperative," insisted Grant, his patience beginning to wear thin. At that moment, Miller asked Grant if he could have a word outside. Both men got up and headed for the door, and as soon as Miller shut the door behind him, he spoke.

"Guv, I don't think she's going to say a lot, so why don't we use her to our advantage?"

"In what way, Graham?"

"While she's in here, we get a wire on her phone. Now once we let her go, I reckon she'll phone our man. It might give us a lead to him or where he is," explained the sergeant.

"We'll need clearance."

"Shouldn't be a problem, sir. I could contact DCI Collins. He'd back it; after all, it could be his man as well."

"Okay, Graham, go for it, go through the proper channels. We can't hold her here forever so we've got to be quick," asserted Grant.

The detective inspector looked on as his sergeant scampered off to do the task. Grant turned to the door and raised his wrist to check the time on his watch. They didn't have much time to act, so Grant would have to play for time.

Grant re-entered the room and again sat opposite the pretty redhead.

"Now shall we start again, Mrs. Jarvis? Or may I call you Marie?" asked the Inspector. Marie shrugged her shoulders, not really bothered.

"I understand you're divorced, Marie, is that right?" began Grant.

"That's correct," replied Marie.

"Any boyfriends at the moment?"

"You're not going to ask me out, are you?" said Marie.

"No, just answer the question, please."

"Shouldn't I have a lawyer or something?"

"You haven't been arrested yet. Have you something to hide, something you don't want to tell me?" asked Grant, glancing at the WPC standing by the door, who looked like a bouncer at a nightclub. "Well, Marie, have you?"

"No, I have nothing to hide."

"So who was it who left your house this morning and drove your car away?" questioned the Inspector once more, this time raising his voice slightly.

"I told you, I don't know what you are talking about," snapped Marie.

"I think you do, Marie. I think you know more than what you are saying," shouted Grant. The effect made Marie sit back and cower away from the raging policeman in front of her. Grant looked at Marie and then at the WPC.

"I'll be back in a while, and I suggest, Marie, that you think about what might happen to you if you get put in prison." Grant left the room slamming the door behind him, all contributing to the act. Grant stood outside the door and smiled, pleased with himself for the way he had pressured Marie Jarvis. Grant headed for the canteen. Twenty minutes, he thought, that should make her stew.

Dempsey had been waiting for two and a half hours when he caught sight of Chalmers. The red Jaguar XJS pulled up across the road from him. Chalmers got out, locked the door behind him, and headed for the building which contained his office.

Dempsey's eyes followed the overweight man until he entered the building. Dempsey looked at his watch; Chalmers would probably be here for the rest of the day, so he would have to just wait around until the time came for him to make his move.

Detective Inspector Grant had returned to the interview room over two hours ago, pressuring Marie to tell more. Marie, though, refused to say anything, which annoyed Grant. Many a criminal had cracked from his questioning by now, but Marie was strong, stemmed on by the thought of Dempsey. She simply clammed up and refused to say anything about the man who left her home this morning.

Grant was just about to wade in with another round of questions when there was a tap at the door, followed by it opening. In the doorway was Detective Sergeant Graham Miller.

"A quick word sir," requested the lower ranked officer. Grant got up and went through the open door, closing it behind him. "All systems go, sir. The phone is wired up for incoming and outgoing calls."

"What did the DCI say about it all?" asked Grant.

"All for it, Guv. He set it up," replied Miller.

Grant nodded at his sergeant and returned to the interview room. Marie sat at the desk, sipping at a cold cup of tea.

"Well, Mrs. Jarvis, you're free to go. We've no further questions for you. The WPC will take you home," said Grant, who then turned and walked away.

Marie stood up, amazed that the ordeal was over. She hadn't said a word, yet was being released. The female constable showed her the way out and Marie followed, although a little perplexed. She left feeling as though she had just won something, but she wasn't sure what.

Grant stood and watched as Marie left with the WPC. He then turned to Miller. "While we're here, Graham, I'd like a word with whoever is in charge of the Chinaman's murder. I want to have a look at his clothes and personal belongings."

"I think it's DI Briggs. I'll go and have a check with the desk officer," answered Miller, who quickly disappeared.

Grant spotted a vending machine down the corridor and headed for it, fishing in his pockets for loose change, but all he had was pound coins. When he reached the machine he decided on a hot chocolate with sugar. As soon as he put the money in the slot, he knew he had been ripped off, because a cup dropped down after half the liquid had already been released. After mumbling to himself about that, he pressed the button for his change. Nothing happened. Grant tried it again, still nothing happened. He slapped the side of the machine, hoping to get a response. Still nothing happened.

"Fucking thing," Grant muttered just as Miller rounded the corner, flanked on his right by a tall, elegant, well-dressed man.

"Guv, this is DI Briggs. He's in charge of the Chinaman's murder investigation," said Miller.

"Please to meet you. Peter Grant," said the inspector as both men shook hands.

Briggs was indeed a tall man. At six-feet-seven, he towered over both Grant and Miller.

"How is it I can be of assistance?"

"I was wondering if we could have a look through the Chinaman's personal belongings," said Grant.

"I can't see what harm it will do since we have nothing to go on. Follow me and I'll show you where they are,' replied Briggs, who immediately began to walk away. Grant and Miller followed, both having difficulty keeping up with the tall policeman, as his long strides ate up the corridor.

Soon they entered a room which looked as though it was only being used for the storage of clothes and personal belongings.

"These are all his personal bits. We've already been through them so don't worry about touching them. Just leave the room as you found it," said Briggs. He left the room, closing the door behind him.

In front of Grant and Miller was a table which had several polythene bags upon it. The bags all contained something that belonged to the Oriental. There was a pair of trousers caked in blood and excrement; another had a blood-stained pullover; and another contained Chang's jacket, which was also covered with thickly congealed blood, which had began to harden.

A fourth bag contained some personal belongings, which were what Grant wanted to examine. Grant undid the clip which kept the bag closed, and he emptied the contents on the table. A notebook fell to the floor as well as a wallet. Miller picked them up and returned them to the table.

"What are we looking for, Guv?" asked the sergeant.

"Anything. Look at that notebook and see if anything jumps out and hits you...a name or an address...anything," said Grant as he picked up the mobile phone and switched it on.

Miller continued to thumb through the notebook, but nothing struck him, so he put that down and opened Chang's wallet and was surprised to find a wad of money.

"Well, he wasn't hard up," commented Miller to his senior officer.

Grant was engrossed in the mobile phone which he held before him. He was going through the list of numbers stored in the phone's memory. Suddenly he stopped and turned to Miller.

"Do you recognize that number?" asked Grant, holding the telephone up to Miller's eyes.

"That's Brian Short's number. What was this guy doing with it?" exclaimed Miller, quite shocked by the revelation.

"Haven't got a clue, Graham. When we get back to the factory, I want that fat bastard in my office."

"There's nothing in here," said Miller as he tossed the notebook back on to the table. "Anything else in there?"

"There are only five or six numbers in here...copy them down, and we'll check them out," stated Grant as he handed his sergeant the mobile. At that moment, Grant's own mobile began to warble in his inside jacket pocket. The detective immediately removed it from his pocket and pressed the receive call button.

"DI Peter Grant, who is it?"

"Peter,"—Grant recognised the Yorkshire accent straight away—"It's DCI Sean Collins."

"Hello, sir. What can I do for you? My sergeant and I were just about to head for Marie Jarvis's place and join in the surveillance team," declared Grant.

"That's what I'm calling you about, Peter. I want you to head back home. I'm on my way now to Dymchurch to take over the investigation," said Collins.

"What do you mean, take over? This is my case."

"The order's come from above, Peter, I'm sorry. You've done a lot of hard work, and you won't be left out when I write my report. No hard feelings, hey, Peter," said Collins.

The phone went dead, and Grant placed it back in his pocket.

"Trouble, Guv?" asked Miller, wanting to know what the call was about.

"We're off the case, Graham. The top floor has spoken," replied the inspector, the annoyance easy to see on his face. They left for home immediately.

Marie Jarvis had not said a word to the woman police officer on the journey back to her house. Instead, she sat and thought about what had happened. Why did they let her go just like that when they obviously knew Dempsey had been at her house?

Still deep in thought, she did not even realise that she was home when the panda car stopped. Marie headed for her front door, fumbling for the keys in her jacket pocket. She looked around to see not only the panda car pull away, but the curtains of the house across from her bungalow twitching. That must be who grassed on me, Marie thought as she turned the key in the lock waiting for the door to give.

As soon as she was inside, she picked up the telephone receiver and opened an address book which contained Dempsey's mobile phone number. After two or three rings Dempsey answered.

"Hello, who is it?"

"John, it's Marie. The police have been here asking questions, and they dragged me off to the police station," she said hurriedly.

"Marie, calm down. What did they ask you, what did you tell them?"

"I didn't tell them anything, but they knew you had been here. I think a neighbour got in touch with the police, someone who saw you leaving this morning."

"Shit, where are you now?"

"Back home. They let me go. I think I fooled them, John," said Marie, seemingly pleased with herself.

"Marie, I'll be back in the morning—have your bags packed and be ready to go. If anything else happens, call me. Marie...I love you," said Dempsey.

"I love you too, John," replied Marie, a tear appearing in her eye. The phone went dead.

Sixty yards down the road, in a large transit van, sat four policemen, each involved with a piece of complicated equipment.

"Did you get all that, Bob?" asked the first policeman.

"Sure did, did you get the number?" asked the second policeman.

"Yep, mobile phone," a third man replied.

Another of the policemen had already picked up a phone to get in touch with Collins.

"Is that DCI Collins?" asked the surveillance expert.

"Yes, Collins speaking."

"Just to let you know, sir, contact has been made."

"Good, did you get the number?" inquired Collins eagerly.

"More than that, sir. He said he's returning tomorrow morning."

"Right. Stay put, I'm coming down there straight away. Meanwhile, find out from the phone company who owns that number," said Collins, hanging up the phone immediately. The surveillance officer looked at his colleagues.

"The governor said well done, boys," he said. "Wanker."

The news that he was off the case devastated Grant. Never before had he been pulled off a case. For half an hour he had not spoke a word to his sergeant, who was driving them back to their police station in Kent.

"I can't leave it like this, Graham," muttered Grant, the break of silence catching Detective Sergeant Miller off guard.

"Sorry, Guv. I wasn't listening."

"I said we can't leave it like this. Where's that list of phone numbers that you wrote down?" asked Grant, holding out his hand. Miller fished in his jacket pocket for his notebook, and after finding it, he thumbed through the pages with one hand while steering with the other.

"There you are, Guv," said Miller, handing his senior officer the notebook. "What are you going to do?"

"Phone them, that way we'll find out who they are."

"But what about Collins, he said we're..."

"Fuck Collins," interrupted Grant, the very mention of Collins' name causing him to fly into a rage. "I'll show that Northern arrogant bastard."

Miller said no more, trying to sit back as far as he could into his chair. The sergeant had every respect for his senior officer but knew that going against the DCI's word was asking for trouble.

Grant had already retrieved his mobile phone from his pocket and had punched in the first number. The reply was a woman's voice.

"Hello, how can I help you?" said the sexy sounding female.

"To whom and I speaking, please?" asked Grant.

"This is the Sergeant Pepper's Lonely Hearts Escort Agency. My name is Melanie, how can we be of service to you?"

"Terribly sorry, I've got the wrong number," Grant lied and pressed the end of call button. Grant turned to Miller, who was already looking at him.

"Fucking escort agency, or brothel," retorted Grant.

The next three numbers revealed nothing—Chang's wine bar, another escort service, and a bookmakers. Grant was beginning to feel that this was maybe a waste of time; besides DI Short's home and work number there was only one left. Grant punched in the series of numbers and waited for the reply.

"Hello, Leonard Chalmers," came the response.

"Leonard Chalmers, I am sorry, I appear to have the wrong number," said Grant. He turned his mobile off and sat there, deep in thought. Miller again looked at him, wanting to know what his inspector had just found out.

"Well, Guv, any luck?"

Grant turned to his sergeant, perplexed. "Who is Leonard Chalmers, Graham?" asked the inspector with a frown.

Miller looked as perplexed as his senior when the name finally rang a bell. "Isn't he a civil servant or something, quite high up?" answered the sergeant, not entirely sure if he was right or not.

"If he's a top civil servant, why does a man who has supposedly murdered three men have his personal phone number?" asked Grant, throwing the question in the air like a teacher would in a classroom.

"Perhaps this Chalmers is a dodgy bastard, Guv. Who knows, he might even be behind it all," said Miller, hazarding a guess.

"When we get back, check him out, home address, where he works, everything. I'll be having words with Brian Short. I want to know why his numbers are on a suspected murderer's phone."

Leonard Chalmers sat at his desk, wondering about the wrong number that he had just had. Somewhat a paranoid man, Chalmers always found it hard to believe that any call was just a wrong number. He always looked more deeply into such matters than necessary. If his phone rang at home but went dead when he picked up the receiver, he would think someone was checking to see if he was home or not.

His paranoid thoughts left him when he heard the knock at his door.

"Come in," said Chalmers. His shapely secretary entered, holding a file in her hands.

"Thank you, Alison. That'll be all for now."

The pretty, dark-haired secretary nodded and left the room.

Chalmers opened the file and read what he wanted to read. After a couple of minutes, he closed the file, picked up the telephone receiver, and dialed the number he had just read in the dossier. After five rings the other end was picked up.

"Hello?" answered the voice at the other end.

"Is that you, Max? It's Leonard Chalmers."

"Year, it's Max."

"Good, I've got a job for you, Max," said Chalmers.

Chapter Nineteen

Dempsey had now been waiting for almost five hours. He tried to cover his conspicuousness by walking up and down the road, first on one side then on the other. Dempsey looked at this watch, and it was almost four o'clock. The wait had made him irritable, and he was becoming more and more impatient. Chalmers never worked later than five; soon, Dempsey would have him.

The hitman recalled that he had not heard Chalmers put an alarm on the Jaguar car. Dempsey surveyed the street. There were not many people around. Would anyone notice him breaking into Chalmers' car? He thought not and approached the elegant piece of machinery.

From his pocket, Dempsey recovered a small pouch which contained some small tools. Before he began breaking into the car, he leaned on the bonnet, checking if there was an alarm or not. No noise or blaring sounds came from the car, so he continued with his action. Dempsey found the break-in quite easy. The door gave a sharp crack as the lock was slipped and he was done. Again looking around, Dempsey clambered into the back seat, shut the door, and locked it. He crouched as low as he possibly could behind the front seats; all he had to do now was wait.

As soon as he arrived back at the police station, Grant summoned Short to his office. Meanwhile, Miller got on with checking out Chalmers. Short was in the canteen, and Grant was made to wait for him to return. Every minute Grant was kept waiting was another minute that his anger intensified.

After waiting for ten minutes, Grant heard the rap on the office door that he was expecting. Short entered the room, wearing rolled up shirt sleeves and a loosened tie, which had stains on it of what he had just eaten.

"What's up, Guv?" enquired the disheveled policeman.

"I was hoping you could tell me, Brian. Shut the door, will you?"

Short shut the door behind him and sat opposite his senior officer.

"How many Chinese men do you know, Brian?" asked the inspector, his face as straight as a die.

"Only the bloke down the Golden Palace, Guv," replied Short, laughing at his own remark. Grant found little to laugh at.

"I suppose you heard about the men who were killed down Dymchurch way," said Grant, searching for a reaction.

"Yeah, don't know what the country's coming to...people getting shot...after all this isn't New York, is it?" said Short, his spirits still apparently quite high.

"One of them was Chinese," stated Grant, still looking for a reaction from Detective Constable.

Short said nothing. Instead, he continued to look at the inspector.

"You see, while I was down that way today, Brian, I had a quick look through this Chinaman's belongings, just on the chance that something might come up."

Short continued to look at Grant; deep down, he knew what was coming.

"Graham and I were going through his things when we noticed his mobile phone. We had a look at the numbers and guess what?"

"What, Guv?" asked Short hesitantly.

"We found your home and work number. How can you explain that?" questioned Grant, who had stayed reasonably calm. Short continued to look at Grant, searching for an answer, but nothing would come out.

Grant could see that Short had no explanation. "Well, Brian, can you explain why a suspected triple murderer has the home and work number of a detective constable?" asked Grant again his anger becoming more and more apparent.

"I, I, I don't know, sir," stuttered the DC, sweat beginning to appear on his forehead.

"Bullshit!" shouted Grant, now standing and pointing his finger at the Constable. "You knew him, now who was he?" The raised voice of Grant caused a few heads to be raised outside the closed office door, each one wondering who was getting a bollocking from the tough, no-nonsense inspector.

Short bowed his head and began to weep,. His career was over. If they knew about Chang, next would be his drug problem.

"Who the fuck was he, Brian?" Tell me," snarled the inspector, realising that Short was on the verge of confessing what he knew.

Short looked up at the Inspector, tears rolling freely down his face. "His name was Robert Chang, he supplied drugs, was used to sort people out, that kind of thing."

"What do you mean...sort people out?" asked the inspector, still angry at what he had learnt.

"He was a paid killer," stated Short, who had now stopped crying.

"For who, Triads?"

"Anyone who was willing to pay, Triads, the IRA, even the government," confessed Short.

"How did you get mixed up with him?" asked Grant, who had calmed down by now.

"Like I said, he was a drug dealer. He gave a good price."

"You mean you're an addict!" said Grant, shocked by the confession.

"For about four years, couldn't get enough of the stuff. Chang supplied at a good price."

Grant was indeed shocked by what Short had said. He hadn't expected anything like this. He dropped back into his chair, stumped as to what to ask the detective constable next. Short broke the silence.

"What happens now, Guv?" he asked regretfully.

"There'll have to be an investigation, and you'll probably be removed from the force. I better have your warrant card, because you're officially suspended from duty," said Grant, who didn't like what he had to do even though the situation warranted the actions he was taking. Short stood up, removed his warrant card from his back pocket, and gave it to Grant.

"I'm sorry, Brian, but that's the way it has to be. I want you in here tomorrow at nine o'clock for a statement," said Grant in a sorrowful voice.

"I'll be here. See you tomorrow, Guv," said Short as he left the room.

Grant remained seated and massaged the bridge of his nose. Today was turning out to be a right bastard and he had just about had enough of it.

Miller entered the room with a file in his hand and saw that Grant was looking a little bit pissed off.

"What did Shorty have to say about his phone numbers, Guv?" asked the sergeant.

"You wouldn't believe it Graham. I'm still wondering if I'm being wound up. The Chinaman was definitely Robert Chang, supposedly a professional hitman and also Brian Short's drug supplier."

"You're fucking joking," responded Miller, his reply showing his shock at the news.

"Do I look like I'm joking?"

"Brian Short on drugs? He's pulling your leg, surely."

"Well he didn't say much when I suspended him," said Grant. "Anyway, what did you get on Chalmers?"

"Well, Guv, I knew the name rung a bell. He got done for drunk driving six years ago in the west end, and that's where I was stationed then. I remember him kicking up a right stink, saying how high and mighty he was, when all along he was only a well-paid civil servant," replied Miller

"Got his address?" asked Grant.

"Home and work, Guv."

Grant glanced at his watch. It was almost four-thirty. "If we put our foot down, we might still catch him at work."

Both men left at a canter.

Ever since breaking into the car, Dempsey had a compulsive urge to keep looking at his watch. When the hell was Chalmers going to leave his office and go home? The position in which Dempsey was crouched was not doing his back any good either. Twice he moved and felt twinges forcing him to assume another posture.

At five o'clock Leonard Chalmers finally opened the door and put his attache' case on the passenger seat. Dempsey lay there patiently, waiting to pounce the moment the car door closed.

As soon as Chalmers closed the door, Dempsey sat bolt upright.

"Don't fucking move," ordered Dempsey, his patience finally rewarded.

Chalmers froze, not knowing what to do. His eyes went to the rearview mirror, wanting to know who it was.

"You scared the life out of me, John!"

"You're lucky I didn't blow your fucking head off," said Dempsey, letting Chalmers feel the Desert Eagle gun against his head. Chalmers felt the coldness of the pistol and shivered.

"Why did you set me up?"

"Come one, John. You know you're just a pawn in a large game of chess. Like everyone, you're replaceable," replied Chalmers, still feeling the cold steel at the side of his head.

"So are you, Leonard," said Dempsey.

"Look, John, I'm sure this can be sorted out. If you want more money, I can authorise that," begged Chalmers.

"I don't want more money, I want the bastard who set me up."

Chalmers sensed the anger in Dempsey's voice, his eyes flitting from the road ahead to the rearview mirror.

"Right, Chalmers, drive. If you try anything, I'll kill you there and then, got me?"

Chalmers nodded. "Where we going?"

"Your house," replied Dempsey instantly.

Chalmers reacted to the answer by trying to turn around, but he was met by the barrel of the three pound weapon that Dempsey held in his hand. Chalmers decided to just get on with it.

As Dempsey lowered the pistol and pointed it at Chalmers' side, the civil servant started the car up and pulled away.

"Why my house, John?"

"You'd rather die in your own house, wouldn't you?" answered the assassin. The answer caused Chalmers to swallow hard. He didn't ask anything else because he was afraid of what he might hear.

Brian Short left his car at the police station, knowing he wouldn't be able to concentrate while trying to drive through London, and he decided on the train, instead. While he walked to the train station, he thought of the good times he had had as a policeman.

Seventeen years Short had been in the force: he knew nothing else except feeling collars. The last few years had been tough, though. When he was rejected for detective sergeant, he had resigned himself to the fact that he would be a detective constable for the rest of his days. That day all ambition had left him, and he simply just settled for it.

When at a party one night he was offered some cocaine, he first turned it down, but eventually gave in. From that night, he had been hooked and wanted as much as he could get. When he heard about Robert Chang, he met him and they made a deal: Short would get the white powder at a discount price if he supplied information to Chang when he needed it. Short agreed, thinking only about the cocaine, but when Chang began to telephone him for the slightest thing, Short realised he was at Chang's command.

Short sat on the bench at the platform, pondering what was left for him. An investigation might even connect him with the crimes that Chang had committed. He couldn't handle a stint inside. There were people in there because of him; he'd be looking over his shoulder every five minutes.

He needed drugs as well. How would he be able to afford the habit he had created over the last three years without a job? Even if he did not go to prison, he refused to become a poxy security guard working for pittance money.

Short leaned forward and placed his head in his hands; deep down he knew what he was going to do. He sat up, wiped a tear away from his eye, and looked up at the platform clock, which continued to clack as every second passed. The next train was due in one minute, according to the piece of equipment hanging next to the clock. As he stared at the clock, a woman sat next to him on the bench. Short looked at her, and she smiled. Short replied with a smile of his own, the tears beginning to well in his eyes as he raised himself from the bench.

Two hundred yards or so away, Short saw the incoming train. He had made his decision and began to walk to the edge of the platform. He glanced behind him, seeing the woman was in the early stages of unwrapping a chocolate bar.

The train was now only a hundred yards away and slowing. With his eyes fixed on the train, Short jumped down onto the tracks, positioning himself so he was looking at the oncoming train.

The train driver spotted Brian Short on the line, sounded a horn, then began to brake. As he took a deep breath, Short ignored the cries and shouts of the onlookers that were telling him to move. Short opened his arms out wide, as though he was meeting the huge mechanical beast with a loving hug. The rolling mass of metal bore down on him, as every second was counted by the platform clock, which clacked away endlessly.

The train driver realised his warnings were having no effect, and braking the train at less than fifty feet had been pointless.

As the train got nearer, Short took in one last deep breath and then shouted at the top of his voice.

Short felt nothing, the impact killing him instantly. His rib cage and skull were crushed as he first went backwards and then got pulled underneath the mechanical beast. People began to scream and shout when they realised exactly what had just happened.

The wheels of the train dragged Short twenty feet before stopping. His right arm was severed just below the elbow, and his right let was completely mangled.

Short had wanted to die and had found a way to do it.

Chapter Twenty

Grant and Miller arrived at Chalmers' office at 5:25. After checking that they were at the right place, they entered the six-storey building and approached the reception area, where a heavily built security guard was stationed.

As they came nearer, the guard stood up from the seat and showed the full extent of his muscular frame.

"Can I help you, gentlemen?" asked the guard, his Cockney accent coming over like a bad impression of Michael Caine.

Grant felt his inside pocket for his warrant card and displayed it to the guard, who immediately backed off from doing his 'you're not allowed in here' routine.

"I'm DI Grant, this is DS Miller, we've come to see Leonard Chalmers."

"Too late, gentlemen, I'm afraid. He left a little while ago. I assume he was going home," said the burly security guard, who had now popped a mint into his mouth.

Grant thanked the guard for his help and left with his sergeant. Since plan A had failed, they would try plan B, and go to Chalmers' home in west London.

During the journey to Chalmers' house, Dempsey had held the Desert Eagle pistol at his employer's side, and did Chalmers know it. Dempsey had pushed the barrel of the gun into his side on numerous occasions, just to let him know that if he was thinking of trying anything on, don't.

Chalmers' house was large, but otherwise ordinary. Situated in one of the more expensive areas of the West End it had suited his and his wife's needs for the last eighteen years.

Chalmers drove as normal up the short drive to the garage. By remote control, he opened the garage door, and the car entered.

"Is anyone in the house, Chalmers?" asked Dempsey.

"No, my wife's away at her sister's," answered Chalmers, waiting for the next order from his abductor.

"Carefully get out and lay on the floor," ordered Dempsey, thinking that if Chalmers was on the floor then he couldn't try anything.

"Are you mad? This is a four hundred pound suit."

Dempsey interrupted the protests by slamming the Desert Eagle pistol into the side of Chalmers' head, momentarily dazing his employer. Chalmers did as he was told.

Dempsey clambered out after him, accidentally pulling out a few of the stitches that were in the wound in his shoulder. After Dempsey got out of the car, he ordered Chalmers to get up. He did, still rubbing the side of his head.

Chalmers' garage had an adjoining door to the kitchen, and this was where Chalmers attempted to make a move but was just too old and unfit. As he entered the adjoining door, he tried to close it quickly behind him, but from a combination of Chalmers' lack of speed and Dempsey's nimbleness, the move failed.

All Dempsey did was give the door a weighty push, which sent Chalmers sprawling to the floor in a heap.

"You want to be careful of that suit, Leonard. Now get up, you fat fuck," said Dempsey through clinched teeth as he grabbed his victim by the lapels and pulled him up.

"Rope, I need some rope," demanded Dempsey.

"There's a ball of string underneath the sink. That's all I have," muttered Chalmers.

"Get it."

Chalmers walked over to the kitchen unit that contained the sink and retrieved from underneath the ball of string. Dempsey noticed something else that he sought was below the sink.

"That bowl as well," said Dempsey.

Chalmers walked back towards his captor with the large plastic bowl and string.

"On the table, Chalmers," requested Dempsey. "Now put the kettle on."

Chalmers did everything Dempsey wanted. He was scared but was unable to fathom out the plan that his abductor was concocting. String, a bowl, a kettle, where would all this lead?

"Now sit down and take your shoes and socks off," instructed Dempsey.

Chalmers sat down on one of the dining chairs in the kitchen and commenced following the order that he had been given. Chalmers looked up at Dempsey, totally flummoxed, and when he finished, he sat back in the chair.

"Hands round the back," ordered Dempsey. His captive did so, and Dempsey took the string and tied Chalmers' wrists tight, causing Chalmers to grimace when the skin was pinched.

"Feet together."

Again Chalmers did what he was told, and Dempsey tied the ankles together with the string, which he had wound around three or four times.

Bound to the chair, Chalmers was totally at Dempsey's mercy. He still had not figured out what was in store for him. Dempsey, though, had it all planned to the last detail.

On a work surface behind Chalmers was a small, portable cassette radio, no doubt for Chalmers' wife to listen to when she was busy in the kitchen. Dempsey removed an audio cassette from his pocket and popped it into the musical appliance.

"What's going on Dempsey? Why bother? I'm not going to tell you anything," exclaimed Chalmers, wriggling a little.

"Shut up and don't move." The statement was said in conjunction with the Desert Eagle pistol pointed at him. Chalmers stopped and looked on.

Dempsey tipped Chalmers and the chair backward slightly, then dragged him to the kitchen unit which had the radio cassette player on it and propped him up so his feet were eight inches from the floor. Chalmers now began to realise what was going on.

Dempsey pressed the record and play buttons on the cassette player, then retrieved the bowl from the table and positioned it below his feet.

"Now then, Leonard, who gave the order for Webster's death?" questioned Dempsey. Chalmers, unaware of the recording being made, gave an answer.

"You know I can't tell you that, Dempsey."

By this time the kettle had boiled and was billowing with steam. Dempsey collected the kettle from the side and approached Chalmers, who, fully aware of the boiling liquid, gave Dempsey a stern look. The former SAS man dropped to his haunches and poured some of the boiling liquid into the bowl, causing Chalmers to frown, the hot steam rising up to the soles of his feet.

"Once again...who gave the order for Webster's hit?" said Dempsey, glaring at the trussed man in front of him.

"I won't tell you."

"Okay," said Dempsey. He picked up one of Chalmers' socks and stuffed it into the captive's mouth. While Chalmers thrust his head from one side to the other, Dempsey maneuvered himself to the side.

In one quick movement, Dempsey pushed the chair forwards, Chalmers' weight tipping it back onto all four legs. Chalmers screamed as his bare feet made contact with the boiling hot water. Chalmers' feet were only in the lot liquid for two seconds, but it seemed longer to him as the pain became excruciating. Dempsey then pulled the chair back to its tilted position.

The pain was evident on Chalmers' reddening face. Dempsey again took the kettle and poured some more boiling water into the bowl. As he poured, he noticed that Chalmers' feet had already began to blister, the now scarlet skin had even began to peel in places.

Dempsey then removed the sock from his captive's mouth, and a strand of saliva stretched from the sock to Chalmers' mouth like the spinning thread from a spider. Dempsey glanced at the cassette recorder, reassuring himself that it was still recording.

"Who gave the order for Webster's hit, Leonard?" again came the question from Dempsey.

Although the pain raked through him, Chalmers was not going to concede. "I can't tell you."

Immediately Dempsey stuffed the sock back into Chalmers' mouth, causing Chalmers to shake his head around. The same procedure as before then followed—the chair went forward and in went Chalmers' feet. Even with the sock muffling his screams, it could be heard he was in serious pain.

Dempsey returned the chair to two legs and glanced at Chalmers' feet. Both were now bright red, and layers of skin had disappeared revealing sore-looking flesh. Fragments of skin were quite visible in the water in the bowl.

Dempsey grasped Chalmers' head and removed the now wet, sputum-stained sock from his mouth. Chalmers was near to passing out.

"For the last time, who ordered the hit on Webster?" enquired Dempsey.

Chalmers was now crying, the tears cascading across his cheeks like lava flowing from a volcano. He could not stand any more of the pain; his feet hurt so much, he had to tell.

"Campbell ordered the hit, Peter Campbell," conceded Chalmers.

Dempsey was surprised that he had given in so quickly, because Chalmers had always come across as a tough, no-nonsense man. Dempsey's illusions of him quickly evaporated.

Why would Campbell, the home secretary, want a cabinet colleague dead? Dempsey had no idea, except that maybe he saw him as a national threat. Maybe Webster was a spy? Dempsey didn't care; now he knew who had set him up.

The assassin looked at Chalmers, who was a sniveling wreck, trussed up in a chair. He now had to decide what to do with him, whether to kill him or let him live. In his present state Chalmers looked a sad man, but Dempsey could not forget what he had done previously.

Dempsey's thoughts were quickly disturbed when the doorbell rang. He looked at Chalmers, who suddenly was alive again. Chalmers began to shout and bellow, crying for help from whoever was at the front door. Dempsey then heard words which caused him to spring into action.

"Police, open up," yelled Grant through the letter box.

Those three words convinced Dempsey what he had to do. He picked up the Desert Eagle pistol and quickly walked over to Chalmers. The second the barrel of the gun was at Chalmers' temple, the trigger was pulled. The 11.17mm bullet ripped through Chalmers' head, causing blood and the interior of his head to decorate the kitchen wall like a bad Picasso. The force of the shot caused Chalmers body to topple from the two legs of the chair on its side. Blood gushed from the entry and exit wounds, a large crimson puddle appearing around his head. At first, the body convulsed as the nervous system tried to live on while the brain was dying. Eventually the twitching stopped. Chalmers was dead.

The sound of the gunshot had convinced Grant and Miller to return to their car and call for back-up. On the radio, Miller explained just who they were and where they were.

Meanwhile in the house, Dempsey had collected the audio cassette from the recorder and was looking for a way out. He returned to the garage and got in the Jaguar XJS; fortunately, Chalmers had left the keys in the ignition from earlier.

The former soldier took the remote control from the dashboard and got ready to open the garage door. The Jaguar's engine roared into life at the turn of the ignition key. Dempsey put the car into reverse gear, pointed the remote control at the garage door, and pressed the button. As the door began to rise, Dempsey got ready to go.

Dempsey floored the accelerator, the wheels spinning on the concrete floor of the garage as they sought traction. They soon found it, and the car suddenly propelled itself backwards. Dempsey, in total control, spun the car when it reached the road.

To his right, he saw Grant and Miller at their car, and he sped past them. The two policemen clambered into their own machine in order to give pursuit. The Jaguar, though, had already built up a large gap between them, and Dempsey's overtaking of the slower traffic gave him an advantage.

The two policemen still had him in sight as they, too, weaved through the traffic, a portable blue light on their dashboard flashing manically as they gave pursuit. As Miller drove, Grant spoke into the radio trying to give details of where they were; as this was not his neck of the woods, he found this quite difficult.

Dempsey's speed never relented. He pulled further away from the police vehicle as every second passed. He now believed he was far enough in front to try and lose them. On his left was an oncoming turning, and as he steered the car to the left, he braked. The backend stepped out, giving the impression of a rally car in fullflow. As he continued down the road, his eyes fixed on the rearview mirror, where he saw the flashing blue light fly past. Dempsey parked the car and got out, making sure he still had the tape on him. When satisfied, he jogged down the road in an attempt to make himself elusive.

Grant and Miller had by now realised that they had lost their prey. Grant threw the radio receiver back towards the dashboard, knowing he had been beaten.

"Fuck, fuck, fuck!" exclaimed Grant. Miller slowed down to normal driving speed and was looking at Grant, waiting for the next order.

"We better get back to Chalmers' house," said Grant. Miller swung the car around, and they returned to the house.

Grant now had to involve Collins, and that would probably mean a bollocking for disobeying orders. The detective inspector sat quietly on the return to the house, as he searched through his thoughts and built up the courage to speak to Collins.

Chapter Twenty-one

We can be heroes, just for one day.
– David Bowie

When Grant and Miller returned to Chalmers' house, there was already a gathering of police cars. Grant got out of his car and approached a police constable who was waiting by the entrance to the drive. As Grant and his sergeant got nearer, the constable began to approach them.

Grant reached in his pocket, as did Miller, both producing their warrant cards. The constable accepted who they were and didn't stop them as they neared the front door.

"Constable," shouted Grant, "get that front door down now!"

The young PC scampered off to get some fellow officers. Grant turned to Miller, who was busy watching the convergence of flashing blue lights in the street.

"Graham, get in touch with Collins and tell him what's happened, tell him that I'll explain everything, that you were acting under orders from me."

"Cheers, Guv," replied the detective sergeant.

As Miller walked away, two men passed him and approached Grant.

"Peter, a bit out of your way, aren't you?" said John Bush. "This is DS Tony Mackenzie." Bush pointed to the man next to him. Grant and Mackenzie exchanged pleasantries as three more uniformed officers came up the drive.

"So what's going on then, Peter?" asked Bush, his face reddening from the chilly breeze.

"We were following up a lead on the Lomax killing, and it brought us here," explained Grant.

"I thought you were off that case," came the reply from Bush.

"Officially we are, Graham's getting in touch with Collins now."

"So what happened here, then?" enquired Bush.

"We knocked on the front door, next thing we heard was a gunshot. We called it in, then all of a sudden the garage door opened and out shot a car. We gave chase but lost him."

"We best have that door down then, hadn't we?" remarked Bush, who then gave the order for the uniformed officers to commence knocking the door down. After three hefty shoulder barges from the trio of policemen, the door gave way, the frame splintering and the door hanging on a hinge.

Bush entered first with Grant immediately behind him, and Mackenzie followed the pair. Bush opened the first door he came to, but it let to nothing except a dark room. Grant was luckier: As he opened the kitchen door, he saw the mass of blood that was now congealing on the wall. On the floor was Chalmers, his head totally destroyed by the blast of the Desert Eagle pistol.

"In here," Grant cried. The other two policemen entered the room, but Mackenzie turned away from the corpse and left the room retching.

"Fuckin 'ell," came a remark from Bush, who was quite visibly shocked by the mess on the wall and on the floor.

"Look at his feet...he's been tortured," said the Kentish policeman.

Bush glanced at the feet and had to control his own stomach. Chalmers' feet had now blistered grotesquely, some of the blisters oozed bloody fluid.

At that moment, Graham Miller entered the room.

"DCI Collins will be here as soon—" Miller's speech was halted by the sight in the room. "Fuck me."

"Tell Mackenzie to get SOCO down here, will you? Have everything cordoned off. You know the procedure," said Bush.

Miller left the room, leaving the two inspectors alone with the corpse.

"So who was he, then?" asked Bush to Grant.

"Leonard Chalmers, as far as I know. Top civil servant, well in with government ministers, apparently," answered Grant. "My bet is he was killed by the same man that killed Lomax and Webster, and I reckon he had something to do with it," said Grant, his head nodding at Chalmers.

"Sounds a bit like guess work to me, Peter," suggested Bush.

"Call it a hunch, call it what you like, but I'm certain."

Miller returned and informed them that SOCO were on their way. Bush decided to have a closer look at the body of Chalmers and slipped in the puddle of blood that had accumulated on the floor around him. After swearing to himself and putting on a pair of rubber gloves, he knelt down and tried (using a biro so he wouldn't touch anything) to get to the inside of Chalmers' jacket.

This he did successfully and eventually reached in and retrieved Chalmers' private diary from his inside pocket. Meanwhile Grant had gone into another room to have a look around, but Bush soon called him back.

"Our friend Leonard here has been involved with some high level meetings lately. Monday at eleven o'clock, P.M. and P.C.; Tuesday at twelve o'clock, R.C. Who do you suppose they are?" questioned Bush.

"R.C. could be Robert Chang, our dead Chinese friend," stated Grant.

"What about P.M. and P.C., and idea on them?" asked Bush.

"No, his secretary might know, though. We could question her," responded Grant, his enthusiasm knowing no boundaries whatsoever.

"You'll question nobody, Grant," said a voice with a broad Yorkshire accent.

Grant knew who it was without even turning around to look. The speed in which Collins had arrived at the murder scene astounded not just Grant, but Bush and Miller as well.

"Do you know the meaning of the phrase, 'You're not on the case anymore'? That was the last thing I said to you, so how do you explain your presence here?" While Collins spoke, his eyes drifted to the stiffening corpse on the floor.

"Alright, I know I'm not on the case anymore, but his man is involved in the Webster assassination," claimed Grant.

"How do you come to that conclusion then, Peter?" said Collins, a sarcastic tone coming through on his voice.

"Show him the diary, John," said Grant. As Collins looked, Grant began to explain. "R.C. is Robert Chang, the Chinaman killed down in Dymchurch. I say Chalmers, under orders from someone higher, issued the hit on Webster."

"So this Chang killed Webster," remarked Bush.

"Not necessarily. I think Chang was after the man who killed Webster," said Grant.

"You'll need more than that, Peter," stated Collins.

Grant wasn't going to give in there, so continued. "What if P.M. and P.C. are Prime Minister and Peter Campbell? What if they ordered the hit?" said Grant, looking at Collins, waiting to see the reaction.

"You're going a bit too far now, come on," answered Collins. This was not the reaction Grant was looking for.

"Someone big had to order that hit, and they don't come much bigger than the prime minister of the United Kingdom," said Grant.

"What do you think, John?" asked Collins.

"I think Peter might have something, could be all to do with politics. Or maybe Webster was getting too big for his boots, so they got rid of him," said Bush.

"Alright, not a word of this goes any further. If you can prove what you are saying, you'll be opening the biggest can of worms that ever existed," stated Collins. "You've got forty-eight hours, that's all I'm giving you. John, you're in as well. I'll tell your guv'ners that you're following up something."

Just as Collins stopped talking, a man walked in the room wearing a dinner suit and carrying a briefcase. Grant told Collins that he would be in touch and left with Bush along side him. Collins stayed and listened to what the coroner had to say.

Outside were Miller and Mackenzie, waiting patiently for their respective senior officers. The two inspectors explained that they were to follow-up some leads and that the two sergeants weren't needed for anything.

As Grant spoke, Collins appeared at the doorway. "By the way, Peter, our suspect is suppose to be meeting up with a girl in Dymchurch tomorrow. I'll keep you informed."

Grant nodded in recognition of the statement. When he returned to his conversation with Miller, his sergeant had moved some twenty feet away and was talking to a uniformed officer.

When Miller finished, he returned to his senior officers and Mackenzie. "Guv, bad news. Brian Short's topped himself."

The news caused Grant to close his eyes and grimace.

"Threw himself under a train, apparently. Must have been on his way home," continued Miller, who bowed his head after saying it.

Grant said nothing, instead closing his eyes and shaking his head. Inside he was too wound up. After all it was he who had just bollocked Short and then suspended him. Grant suddenly felt very guilty.

Chapter Twenty-two

Dempsey made his way back to Marie's car, which he had left near Chalmers' office block, via the bus service. Killing his employer hadn't been a real problem for him, but torturing a man wasn't really his style. Still, it had made Chalmers talk and Dempsey had that information in front of him in the form of a small black audio cassette.

Dempsey checked around him before he approached and entered the white Escort. Once in the car, he decided to check the cassette, make sure everything was on there before the next part of the plan would take place.

He pushed the cassette in to the player and listened, nothing. Panic suddenly came over the assassin as he ejected the tape and inspected it. Dempsey then realised that it hadn't been rewound. For a few seconds, he had thought that torturing and finally killing Chalmers would have all been in vain. He returned the cassette to the player and pushed the rewind button, and the machine started to buzz as it rewound the small piece of tape.

As it rewound, Dempsey looked in the rearview mirror, and he made out what looked like one of the men who was outside Chalmers' house. The man was going into the offices where his former employer worked. The hitman decided it was time to move on, just in case he was spotted or recognised. Dempsey rescued the cassette from the recorder, which had now stopped buzzing, and returned the cassette to his inside pocket.

Under the guidance of Dempsey, the white Escort pulled away from where it had been parked. As he passed the entrance, he slowed a little, to see if he could see anything. The policeman was at the front desk gesticulating at a guard who was stationed there. Dempsey sped up and moved on, out of arms reach.

Grant had showed the guard, who was different from the earlier guard in every way, his warrant card, and had asked to see Chalmers' office. The guard, doing everything by the book, flatly denied the policeman his request. Grant found this hard to take and asked for a person of seniority. As they waited for the security manager to appear, Grant paced up and down, the way an expectant father would. He glanced at the security guard every so often, and wondered how a man who weighed probably no more than eight stone would be able to stop anyone trying to breach security. The earlier guard had looked the part, but this man probably wouldn't be able to fight his way out of a paper bag.

As Grant continued his thoughts, a man appeared from a door that was behind the desk. He spoke to the security guard as Grant looked on and waited. The policeman was annoyed when the senior man came over to him.

"I understand you want admittance to one of the offices," said the man in a voice that sounded like he had a plum in his throat.

"That's right, Leonard Chalmers. He was murdered this evening, an investigation is under way, and I need to look at that office," replied Grant, his voice coming over a little harshly.

"I'm sorry Mr. Chalmers is dead, but I cannot admit you to that office."

"Why not? This is a police investigation," emphasized the policeman.

"There are government papers in that office. I can't just let anyone in there. You'll have to go through the correct procedure. If he wasn't murdered here, then I believe this is not a crime scene, is it, Inspector?" said the plummy voice, smiling.

Grant looked at him, and the words "you fucking smug bastard" entered Grant's head, but he didn't say them. Instead he turned and walked away, only to stop before he opened the door.

"You haven't heard the last of this, I can assure you," bellowed Grant, his index finger pointing at the senior security officer. On that Grant turned and left.

Dempsey had stopped the Escort in a lay-by about three miles from Chalmers' offices. From the glove compartment, he removed a padded envelope and a pen. Next to him was one of the daily newspapers, opened at a page which had DCI Sean Collins' photo on it. Dempsey could not remember who was in charge of the investigation so had bought a newspaper to remind him. He knew the story of the foreign secretary's assassination was still headline news, so the newspaper was a cheap source of information for him.

Dempsey copied the name onto the envelope and addressed it to New Scotland Yard. He also had a stamp with him and stuck it in the top right-hand corner. Dempsey pushed the cassette into the envelope and licked the foul tasting glue on the back to seal it together.

Opposite was a pillar box; Dempsey opened the car door and jogged across the road. Before he pushed the envelope into the hole, he checked for the emptying times, and the next was eight-thirty in the morning. Dempsey smiled. We'll be on our way to France by then, he thought as he pushed the small package into the gaping mouth of the red pillar box.

Dempsey jogged back to the car muttering, "Get out of that, Campbell."

Dempsey glanced at his watch. It said eight forty-five, so Dempsey decided to get some sleep before he returned to Marie's. Tomorrow would probably be a long day, so rest was essential. No one would notice him if he parked in an alley to get some sleep. Tomorrow he would be with Marie, and they would go to France and start a new life together—away from England and away from the police.

Chapter Twenty-three

By the time Grant had returned to Chalmers' house, SOCO was busy doing its thing. Neighbours were still being interviewed by the uniform brigade and some detectives. As Grant pulled up in the Mondeo, he saw his counterpart in the shape of DI John Bush, who was standing outside the house smoking a cigarette.

Grant parked the car and approached Bush, ducking underneath the police tape as he entered the gardens of the house. Bush flicked the cigarette from his hand to the floor and squashed it into the ground with his foot.

"Did you get anything, Peter?" asked Bush, rubbing his hands together. It had turned in to quite a chilly night.

"Only a pompous wanker who wouldn't let me into Chalmers' office. You must take the correct procedure, you know," answered Grant, the last part of the answer delivered with a hint of sarcasm.

"So what now?"

"I'll call Collins and let him know how I got on. I think we should have a chat with Peter Campbell, see what his reaction is," replied Grant. "SOCO come up with anything?"

"Plenty of prints. They think one of them's our man, whose prints have been everywhere."

Grant nodded in recognition as he got the mobile phone from his pocket and punched in the numbers for Collins. The phone rang, but there was no reply. Where could Collins be? Grant pressed the end of call button and turned to John Bush, who had lit up another cigarette.

"No answer on his mobile," said Grant. He looked unsure as to what to do next. Should he contact Collins before questioning Campbell, or should he get on with it? Fuck it—he was a detective inspector, why should he go asking about what he should do next?

"Right, let's see Campbell and see what his reaction's like," state Grant. Bush nodded in agreement.

Bush had a word with Mackenzie, giving him instructions and letting him know where he and Grant were going. As soon as Mackenzie was sure he knew everything, the two detective inspectors left.

After Grant had phoned around, they traced the home secretary to his gentlemen's club in Westminster. Bush had been there before to question someone two years ago, but Grant was surprised at how chauvinist it was. NO WOMEN PERMITTED IN THE CLUB, said a sign at the entrance.

On entering, they were met by a surly-looking man wearing a very old fashioned uniform.

"Yes, gentlemen, may I be of assistance?" asked the uniformed man politely.

Both Bush and Grant searched in their pockets for their respective warrant cards.

"DIs Bush and Grant," proclaimed Bush. "We understand Mr. Peter Campbell is here. We need to have a word with him."

"He is here. I'll ask him if he is available," said the man, who then walked off a great pace. Grant looked around him as he waited. He didn't think this kind of place existed anymore; paintings on the wall, large vases all probably very expensive.

The concierge returned, looking a little ruffled.

"Mr. Campbell will see you. Follow me, please," he said, then began to walk off. The two policemen glanced at each other and then followed. They followed the concierge down a small corridor and then through a door, where Peter Campbell was sitting, a large cigar in one hand and an equally large glass of brandy in the other. As they approached, the home secretary stood up and held out his hand to greet them.

"Peter Campbell, how can I help you?" he said, shaking both the policemen's hands.

"I'm DI Grant, and this is DI Bush. We were hoping you could answer some questions for us."

"I'll certainly try. Please sit down. I thought it would be more private in here," said Campbell, gesturing to the large leather settee. Both inspectors accepted but declined a drink when Campbell offered.

"Do you know a Leonard Chalmers, sir?" asked Grant, watching for a reaction. None came.

"Yes, a likable chap. I've met him on probably four occasions. May I ask why?" said Campbell.

"He was murdered this evening at his home," replied Grant. This time there was a reaction. The news of Chalmers' death hit Campbell like a brick, he was obviously shocked.

"Murdered, you say?"

"Shot through the head, and he had been tortured as well," said Bush.

"That's outrageous! I hope you got the chap who did it," stated Campbell.

"What makes you think it's a man?" asked Grant quickly.

"I can't imagine a woman doing such a thing, that's why," came Campbell's immediate response. He had a good idea who killed Chalmers but wasn't going to say anything.

Grant continued to look at the politician, and deep down he knew that Campbell was not telling the whole story.

"You say you've met Mr. Chalmers on probably four occasions. Would any of them have involved the prime minister?" asked Bush.

"I believe we had a meeting, yes. About two weeks ago I think."

"Can we ask what that meeting was about?" continued Bush.

Campbell took a large swallow of the brandy before he responded to the question. "Only government business, nothing of any real importance. Signing papers, that sort of thing."

Although he wasn't sure, Grant fired a question at the politician. "According to Mr. Chalmers' diary, you've had nine meetings together over the last two weeks. Seeing how recent these meetings were, I would have thought you would have remembered them." Grant kept his stare firmly fixed on Campbell.

"I didn't realise it was nine. I have so many meetings with so many different people that I must have lost track," explained Campbell, meeting Grant's stare with his own as he answered. Again he took a large gulp of the brandy, finishing what remained in the glass.

"Now gentlemen, unless there are anymore questions, I will say good evening to you." Campbell stood as he spoke, again offering his hand to the policemen. Grant shook the hand and again met Campbell's eyes with his own. "Good evening to you both, and I hope you catch the person who killed Chalmers."

"Oh, we will. I can assure you," replied Grant. On opening the door, the uniformed man from earlier met them and showed them out.

When outside, Grant turned to Bush and spoke. "The bastard's covering something up, I know he is."

"We've got to prove it, though," replied Bush.

"We will. I don't know how, but we will," said Grant, the determination apparent in his voice.

Inside, Campbell had a phone brought to him, and he waited for the waiter to close the door before he dialed the number. The phone rang only once before it was answered.

"May I speak to the prime minister, please? It's Peter Campbell, the home secretary.

Dempsey had found a small alley in which to park, just next to a parade of shops. It didn't take him long to nod off, either, especially after what had happened that evening. He had no regrets about killing Chalmers, none at all.

Chalmers' death was something that Dempsey had vowed to do after Carole and Lisa were murdered. He only had contact with Chalmers when there was a job needed doing, and that was as much as he could tolerate. But after finding out that Chang had lived and Chalmers knew, Dempsey had no more patience and simply waited for the opportunity.

Dempsey was in the back seat of the car, asleep, when he was awakened. At first Dempsey didn't know what was occurring as the car was shaken from side to side, but when he regained his senses, he realised what was happening.

Three men were pushing the car from one side to the other—one of them hurling abuse at Dempsey, the other two laughing in a drunken stupor. Dempsey didn't need this, but three teenage pissheads weren't going to walk over him.

When Dempsey opened the rear door, the three men grouped together, wanting trouble. Dempsey closed the door behind him and surveyed the trio.

One was tall and heavy set, the other two, smaller and thinner.

"Look lads, I'm going to give you the chance to walk away, but if you don't, I won't hold back," warned Dempsey.

"Who do you fuckin' think you are then, Rambo or som'thin'?" said one of the smaller men. The other smaller one had a bottle in his hand, which he held by the neck and smashed it into the wall leaving jagged glass. The bigger one stepped forward and spoke.

"Don't worry, mate, we won't 'urt you too much."

Dempsey shook his head, waiting for the first attack from the three-man gang. The smaller man without the bottle made the first move, charging at Dempsey. Dempsey's superior speed and skill showed immediately as he grabbed the oncoming man and threw him against the car. The teenager, obviously winded, didn't even see Dempsey's next move. Now driven by anger, Dempsey slammed his fist into the man's face, causing blood to erupt from a cut that had opened up under his right eye. The force of the punch caused him to black out.

Dempsey turned to see the man with a bottle bearing down on him, and he got out of the way just as the jagged glass swished past his face. Again the remains of the bottle cut through the air as the teenager aimed at Dempsey. Dempsey waited until the bottle surged forward aimed at his chest. Then he maneuvered himself to the right and grabbed the arm which controlled the bottle.

Standing slightly in front, Dempsey gripped the man's wrist, and thrust his right elbow back towards the man's face. On connection the teenager's nose exploded, and blood mixed with mucous flew through the air. The teenager dropped the bottle as Dempsey released his hold. The teenager's hands covered his face, blood flowing freely through his fingers. Dempsey had not yet finished with him, so dropped down on his haunches and threw a right hand punch to the teenager's genital area. The hurt in his nose suddenly left him as his genitals erupted with pain. He fell to the floor nearing unconsciousness.

The hitman then turned his attention to the largest member of the trio, who had seen what had happened and now seemed apprehensive. Dempsey walked forward, approaching the final member of the gang.

"Come on then, you fucker," rasped Dempsey, his rage out of control, and his intentions obvious.

The teenager then ran at Dempsey, but Dempsey simply repeated the move he had made on the first member of the gang and threw him this time against the wall. The teenager, still surprised by the speed of his opponent, then felt the weight of Dempsey's fists as the first punch struck his face. His top lip inflated the way a rubber dinghy would when being filled with air.

The second punch opened up a cut above his eye, and the third made it larger. Dempsey, ready to throw another, realised the teenager was out on his feet. The hitman released him, and he slumped to the floor. Dempsey had a quick look around him, making certain nobody had heard the fracas. When satisfied, he got back in the car and drove away. He still felt the rage inside him but was calming quickly.

Dempsey glanced at his watch; it was two-thirty in the morning. He'd be back in Dymchurch by four, then he would explain to Marie how they would escape to France, and how eventually they could live a normal life.

As he drove, he realise how much he had gone out of control whilst having that fight. Another day, he would simply have backed out, but this time he had wanted it, enjoyed it, even looked for it.

Dempsey looked at his right hand, which had begun to ache a little. He then realised his index finger was dislocated; he hadn't even felt it, so much was the anger inside him. He stopped at the traffic light which had just turned to red and grasped the finger with his other hand. Within a second, the finger was returned to its normal position, Dempsey broke out in a sweat as the pain rushed through his body.

The light had now turned to green. Dempsey pulled away, his hand throbbing but thoughts of Marie made the pain lessen. Soon they would be together.

Chapter Twenty-four

> Never gonna survive unless we're all a little crazy
>
> – Seal

The time was almost three-fifty when Collins entered the surveillance van, and he looked tired. Ten hours sleep in the last forty-eight hours had done nothing for him. Instead of his usual three piece suit, he was wearing jeans, trainers, a denim shirt, and a leather jacket, the attire more accustomed for a stakeout. He was also armed with an automatic pistol, nestled under his armpit.

"Any sign yet?" enquired Collins to a lower ranking officer.

"None yet, Guv, but everyone's ready," he replied. Next to him were three more officers, each armed and wearing caps with the word police emblazoned across them.

"Give me your radio, will you?" commanded Collins, and one of the officers handed him their radio. Collins took it and pressed the button on the top.

"This is Collins. No one moves unless I say so," he said. The order was short and direct.

There were fourteen men involved in this operation; each was armed and had been briefed to the last detail. Some were to be ready with their weapons; others, though, would be ready with a series of spotlights to give more light on what would be a dark winter's morning. A mistake could not happen—in Collins' mind, would not happen. Catching the murderer of a top politician so quickly would do much to enhance Collins' career. Fucking up would probably mean he would remain a detective chief inspector for the rest of his working life.

"I repeat, nobody moves unless I say so," reiterated Collins.

"Guv, looks like showtime," said one of the officers.

He was right. Dempsey parked the white Escort outside Marie's house and headed for the front door. The door opened before he got there, though. Marie hadn't slept, because she had waited for Dempsey ever since they spoke on the telephone. After they kissed each other, they both entered the house, closing the door behind them.

"We'll wait until they come out. Everybody on standby," said Collins, talking into the black box he had in his hand.

The fourteen police officers weren't the only ones listening to Collins' instructions, though. Some eight hundred metres away, a man sat in a grey Vauxhall, waiting. He fiddled with the police scanner in front of him, something he had been doing for the last two days in various places. It was still early so there weren't many cars around, and he wasn't very conspicuous at all. If he was approached he would say he stopped because he hadn't felt well.

Behind him laying on the back seat, covered with a car blanket, lay the SIG SG 550 sniper rifle, what was almost four feet long, and weighed just over seven kilos, and had a magazine containing thirty shells. Max was very ready, indeed.

Marie was happy to see Dempsey. During the last few hours, her mind had begun to wander, and she had imagined that all kinds of things could have happened to Dempsey. But now he was back with her. She was eager to know what had happened back in London, but the hitman was not too forward in telling her.

"Did you sort it out when you were in London?" she asked

Dempsey was guzzling away at a pint of milk. He wiped his mouth with the back of his hand before replying. "Yeah, it was sorted. Everything was sorted."

"So we don't need to hide anymore."

"We've still got to leave the country. A ferry leaves from Folkestone in a couple of hours so we can't hang around," said Dempsey agitatedly.

"If you sorted it out, why have we got to leave the country?" asked Marie, her voice sounded as if she was near to tears.

"I had to kill Chalmers, and the police were standing outside when I did it," explained Dempsey. His eyes met hers. Marie had began to cry. Just when she thought everything was okay, she had suddenly taken a body blow.

"I'd understand if you didn't want to come with me, you could stay if you wanted."

Dempsey needed Marie now more than anything else. She had given him a reason to find his mind again, a reason to forget Carole and Lisa.

The pretty redhead raised her head and looked at Dempsey, who was waiting for an answer.

"I'll come with you, John. I love you," said Marie. Dempsey smiled and the two embraced and then kissed. Their lips locked together for what seemed like an eternity. Soon, Dempsey thought, we'll be in France.

By now Max had positioned himself. Around six hundred metres away, he lay on a small, concealed knoll overlooking the area that contained Marie's house. The sniper's rifle had already been checked and was ready for action. Max sat there with a pair of binoculars in one hand and a sandwich in the other. As he spied, he ate. Max would not have to wait for long.

Some had felt that Collins' decision to wait for Dempsey to leave the house was the wrong one. Amongst themselves, other officers had talked of storming the small house, eking Dempsey out that way. These police officers were the more gung-ho kind. Collins had planned everything and was now doing it his way.

This way there would not be a possibility of Marie getting accidentally shot by a trigger-happy policeman. This way Dempsey would be taken without a gunfight and without the possibility of a police officer getting shot. Collins was content to do it this way—no risks.

"Guv, we've got movement," remarked one of the officers.

Collins put the radio to his mouth and spoke. "Everyone get ready. Move on my say-so."

The front door opened, and Marie and Dempsey stepped out, each carrying a sports holdall. Dempsey surveyed the street, more out of habit than anything else. Both of them approached the car.

"Go, go, go," bellowed Collins into the radio.

Those three words sent fourteen men into action. Doors from various cars parked along the street opened, and men strode to their various positions. Dempsey realised what was happening, but this time he wasn't quick enough.

"Armed police, do not move," shouted the officer who had appeared about fifteen feet in front of Dempsey.

For a fleeting second, Dempsey thought about going for his gun, but knew he would be dead instantly if he did. By now Collins had appeared, and Dempsey recognised him from the newspaper. Collins looked much bigger in black and white. The spotlights all came on at the same time, emblazoning the front of the house and the small garden with light. Dempsey squinted as the lights shone in his face.

"Hands on your head, now," instructed Collins. Dempsey dropped the sports holdall and glanced at Marie. She was crying.

"Did you know this was going to happen?" asked Dempsey, his face sullen. Marie shook her head.

"I said hands on your head," repeated the leader of the operation. Dempsey looked around him; he was surrounded by armed men and had no other option but to concede to the police.

As his arms rose the first bullet struck. Dempsey's head snapped back as the sniper's bullet hit him in the right eye. The eye exploded on impact, and blood began to stream down in the assassin's face.

"Stop firing!" ordered Collins. His cries were to no avail, though, as the second bullet struck. Already falling backwards, Dempsey was hit in the forehead. He was dead before the back of his head crashed into the pavement.

"Stop firing!" bellowed Collins. Collins looked around him to see the other officers looking around them. Marie was on the pavement, cradling Dempsey's blood-soaked head and crying hysterically.

Collins was still looking around him in a state of shock, his face looked stressed and pained.

"Who opened fire?" he bellowed, his broad Yorkshire accent heightened in the moment of anxiety.

No one replied. No one knew.

Max collected the sniper's rifle and returned it to his car. Lighting the area up like that had only made his job easier. He positioned the rifle in the boot and locked it. He sat in his car and retrieved yet another sandwich from his lunchbox. As he drove away, he munched merrily on ham and cheese.

Flashing blue light, police cars, witnesses being interviewed and, an ambulance; some of the main ingredients of a crime scene. Collins sat in his car in silence. In his mind his career was fucked. Alright, they had tracked Dempsey down, but someone shot him and took all the glory away. As he sat there and felt sorry for himself, a lower ranked officer came over to his car and tapped on the door's window. Collins looked around. With a press of a button the window descended.

"All the firearms have been checked, sir. The shots didn't come from any of our lads," he said.

"Thanks," said Collins with a nod. The news didn't help him, though. His suspect was dead, and he would not have the glory that he had wanted.

Chapter Twenty-five

Collins had contacted Grant around eight in the morning. Grant was shocked to hear that the suspect had been killed right under the noses of a special police squad. Grant could tell by Collins' voice that he was not happy with what had happened. Whilst on the phone, Grant told his superior about the visit to Campbell, and Collins agreed that they had done the right thing by not waiting and getting on with it. After Collins had finished, Grant hung up. He was to meet DI Bush at 8:45 at Chalmers' house, where they would go through some of the dead man's things.

Collins knocked on the office door and waited for the call to come in. When it came, he entered, to be met by a huge man sitting behind a desk. It was Assistant Chief Constable Palmer.

Joseph Palmer was respected by just about everyone in the force. He had started as a constable twenty-four years ago, quickly seizing the opportunity to move higher when it came. Why was he respected? Because he had been there and done it. He knew what a constable was on about when he was complaining, he knew that a station sergeant was a man to be heard and not ignored, and he knew what was bullshit and what wasn't.

Collins sat down opposite his senior officer and waited for the salvo of questions.

"What happened, Sean?" asked Palmer, his Cockney accent just breaking through.

"I really don't know sir. The shots didn't come from any of our officers. We don't know where they came from," replied Collins. "Some of our men have combed the area and have found nothing."

"What kind of bullets were they?" enquired the assistant chief constable.

"Postmortem is being carried out now. Looked like a small caliber, though."

"Professionals?"

"Could be, sir," said Collins, his face still looking pensive.

"A press conference has been arranged for twelve. Don't screw up," stressed Palmer. "Is there anything else I should know?"

"There is a possibility that the home secretary may have some involvement," said Collins warily.

"What! How did you come to that?"

"A diary we found at Chalmers' house has possibly mentioned him."

"You better prove that beyond any doubt. I don't want any scandal, you understand me?" said Palmer.

Collins nodded.

"Now don't forget twelve o'clock."

At seven minutes past twelve Collins entered the press room. He was accompanied by Assistant Chief Constable Palmer and Robert Jenkins, the press relations officer. They approached the long table at the front of the room and sat in the chairs behind their respective name plates. The room fell silent as the three men sat down.

The press were all there. Every major daily newspaper--The Sun, The Daily Mirror, The Times, The Guardian--was represented by one of its journalists.

Collins took a sip of water from a glass that was in front of him and then coughed, clearing his throat. Palmer sat with his hands interlocked on the table, tapping his thumbs together. Again Collins cleared his throat; now he was ready.

"Ladies and gentlemen, at five a.m. this morning, a thirty-eight-year-old man was fatally shot outside a house in Dymchurch. He was the lead suspect in the murder of James Webster. Fifteen officers were involved in the operation including myself," said the Yorkshire officer, his accent rebounding off the walls in what had become a room of silence. "After further investigations, we should be able to conclude that he was the man who killed not only James Webster, but Charles Lomax as well," said Collins. He then looked up, giving the sign for any questions. The Daily Mail reporter raised his hand. Collins acknowledged.

"Do we have a name for the man?" asked The Daily Mail reporter.

"We're not going to release that yet," replied Collins.

The man from The Sun raised his arm, the pencil in his hand pointing up.

"How certain are you that this is the man who killed the home secretary."

"Ninety percent certain. As I said, further investigations will confirm it."

"Can you name the officer who shot him?" asked The Times reporter. Collins took a quick glance at Palmer, who hadn't moved from his position since he sat down.

"At the moment we're not sure who fired the fatal shots," said Collins cagily.

"Hasn't anyone admitted to it, then?" continued the *Times* reporter.

"We think the shots came from elsewhere, not one of the armed officers," said Collins. Many of the reporters suddenly sat up, some looked at each other with puzzled expressions.

"Are you telling us that the assassin of James Webster was assassinated?" commented the Sun journalist.

"We are following up enquiries, and as yet, we do not know where the fatal shots were fired from," said Collins, not really answering the question. The DCI realised that the questions might begin to get a little hot for him to handle, so he stood up. "Thank you ladies and gentlemen, that's as much as I can tell you for now," he said and walked through the door. Palmer followed, leaving Jenkins to sort out what was now a yelling mass of people.

Palmer caught up with Collins just outside. "Good one, Sean. Told them nothing they didn't need to know."

Collins looked at his senior officer, waiting for more. "Tell me, any more news about the possible involvement of Campbell?"

"Nothing yet. Two DIs are following it up."

As soon as you get anything, let me know, immediately. See you later," said Palmer, who then continued to walk down the corridor. Collins suddenly had a thought: If Campbell was involved there may be an attempt to cover it up. That's why Palmer wants to know. Collins took a deep breath. You'll know when you have to, he thought.

Grant met Bush at nine, a little later than arranged, but Bush didn't complain. It gave him a chance to smoke another three cigarettes. The house had had a police guard put on it for now, just in case of any break-ins. Mrs. Chalmers was apparently with her sister, being comforted after being told of her husband's death.

As they opened the front door, they acknowledged the constable who was on guard, entered the house, and were immediately hit by the atmosphere of death.

"So where do we start, Pete?" asked Bush, who was looking up and down the walls and at the ceiling.

"He must have had a study, somewhere to work while he was at home. We'll find that and check through it. We need something that will incriminate Campbell. That bastard is involved, I'll bet my job on it," stated Grant. Bush noticed a certain determination in his voice, something that had been missing the last few days.

After a couple of minutes of searching, they finally came across a small room which contained a desk, some books, and a filing cabinet. Grant motioned to Bush that he had found it and then entered.

"You check the filing cabinet, and I'll go through the desk," said Grant.

Both men set about their business, each looking methodically for a link to Campbell.

"Nothing here, Pete. Just records and receipts, nothing to help us," exclaimed Bush. Bush looked around to find Grant engrossed in, what looked like a journal. "You got something?"

Grant looked up at Bush. "Fucking right we have."

"January sixth, nineteen eighty-eight. PM gives order to eliminate Frank Richards, prominent businessman. January tenth, elimination carried out, total success," read Grant from the journal. Bush stood there, astounded and confused.

"This book is full of dates and orders to have people killed. Here's another." Grant thumbed through the book. "August third, nineteen ninety-one, PM and FS give the order to eliminate Iraqi ambassador to the UN. Mission completed August fifteenth." Grant looked up from the journal to see a worried face on Bush.

"Peter, this is very deep shit we're getting ourselves into. If this gets out, it might bring the government down. We should take it to Collins, see what he says," explained Bush.

"Not until after we see Campbell. The entries are in here for Lomax and Webster. I still say PC stands for Peter Campbell, and if it does, I want him for murder," bellowed Grant. The Kentish policeman rose to his feet and left with the journal firmly in his hand. Bush followed behind, unsure as to whether Grant's tactics were right. The two of them left the house, again acknowledging the constable at the front door. They left for Westminster and to see Peter Campbell.

Peter Campbell relaxed comfortably in the large leather bound Chesterfield chair, which over the last year had become his own. The gentlemen's club in Westminster was as usual quite busy at eleven; businessmen conducting business with other businessmen, elderly men relaxing, and a few members of parliament preparing themselves for the forthcoming day.

When not away on official business, Peter Campbell always prepared his day at the club. With a coffee and maybe a light snack, he would go through the daily newspapers, briefing himself about matters that have occurred not only at home but also abroad.

It was while reading the Times that he read about the death of Leonard Chalmers, and in the stop press, the death of Chalmers' killer. Although disappointed about Chalmers' death, he was quite ecstatic about the death of John Dempsey. He could now put his plans into action, begin to believe in his prospects of becoming the nation's leader.

"More coffee, sir?"

Campbell looked up to see his favourite waiter. "Yes, please, Tim."

"All this killing is awful, sir, isn't it? Not even safe in your own house anymore," commented Tim. Campbell looked the younger man up and down.

"But at least they got him, didn't they?" said Campbell. He noticed that Tim was looking at him quite affectionately. "Could you bring me a telephone please, Tim?"

The waiter walked away, Campbell's eyes following him as he went for the telephone. He smiled when Tim began to return.

"There you are, sir," said Tim, who then bent down next to him to plug the wire in to the wall. As he rose, he brushed the home secretary's leg causing him to smile.

"Thank you, Tim. I'll see you later," said Campbell. He then dialed the number for his office at the Commons.

"Grace, I want you to arrange a press conference for Friday. No clues as to what it is about, arrange it for around one," he said then placed the receiver back in the cradle.

It was then that he heard the commotion coming from the foyer. It was Grant and Bush, forcing their way in to see Campbell. The home secretary was still seated when the two policemen came towards him with the concierge ahead of them.

"I'm sorry, Mr. Campbell, but they insisted," said the concierge.

"That's quite alright, Raymond," said Campbell. He then turned his attention to Grant and Bush. "What is the meaning of all this?"

Grant could see that they had already agitated him.

"Just a couple of questions, sir."

"Could it not have waited? I'm giving a speech in the House in an hour."

"Like I said, just a couple of questions. What do you know of a government department whose only purpose is to kill top businessmen or even cabinet ministers?" asked Grant.

"That's preposterous, Inspector," Campbell said. "I hope you are not implying anything."

Campbell seemed quite set back by the question.

"Not implying anything at all, sir. We found a detailed journal that had been written by Leonard Chalmers. We need to investigate to determine whether it's fiction or fact," said Grant craftily.

"Well I know nothing of it. Now, if you don't mind, I am rather busy," stated Campbell.

Grant stared at him; he knew Campbell was hiding something and was going to prove it.

The two policemen set off to leave, and Grant glanced behind him to see Campbell dialing a number on the telephone.

"Now he's shitting himself," said Grant.

Chapter Twenty-six

At three-thirty both Grant and Bush had been given the order to return to Collins' office at New Scotland yard. Since seeing Campbell dialing frantically on the telephone, Grant had half expected to be called in and probably given a thoroughly good bollocking. Perhaps they should have gone to Collins first and sought his advice. No, fuck it. Why should they have? Collins only would have told them to pack it in and end the investigation. After all, each killing had now been solved in most people's eyes, but not Grant's, because he knew Campbell was dirty and he wanted him badly.

By four o'clock, Grant was walking up the stairs that led to Collins' office, behind him was John Bush. Grant had already told Bush that he would tell Collins that it was all down to him and Bush had only acted under duress.

Before entering the DCI's office, both policemen straightened their ties and adjusted themselves accordingly. Before knocking, Grant positioned the journal under his arm. He then knocked on the door. It was met with a loud "Come in." Collins certainly sounded pissed off. Both men entered, only to be met by three pairs of eyes.

Behind the desk was DCI Sean Collins, to his right was Assistant Chief Constable Joseph Palmer, and by the window standing with his arms crossed was a well-dressed man whom Grant had never seen. Bush closed the door behind him, and both men sat down after being offered chairs.

"Peter, John, this is Assistant Chief Constable Palmer," said Collins. Both policemen looked at their senior officer and nodded in recognition. "And this gentlemen is Daniel Vaughn of MI-5."

Vaughn nodded. Grant, though, returned the greeting with a frown.

"This afternoon we received this through the post," explained Collins, holding up the audio cassette that had been sent by Dempsey. "You should listen to what is on it."

Grant continued to frown, and he looked at Bush, who was just as confused. Collins pushed the cassette into the deck and pressed the play button. Grant continued to look on, first at Vaughn, and then at Palmer. The cassette recorder suddenly began to talk.

"Now then, Leonard, who gave the order for Webster's death?" Grant sat forward, thinking perhaps what he needed to get Campbell was all there.

"You know I can't tell you that, Dempsey."

The next few seconds, all that could be heard on the recording was pouring water. Grant's gaze caught Collins attention, but Collins was straight-faced, even more so than usual.

"Once again, Chalmers, who gave the order for Webster's hit?" continued the recording. Grant listened intently, wanting to hear the answer.

"I won't tell you," said the voice on the tape. "Okay," said the other voice. Grant frowned as the next few seconds contained what sounded like a scuffle, then a muffled scream.

"Okay Sean, wind it forward a little, the next minute or so is more of Chalmers being tortured," commanded Palmer.

Collins pressed the button to wind the tape forward. This it did for about three seconds, then Collins pressed the play button again. Grant continued to listen, waiting for the answer, waiting for the name he wanted to hear.

"For the last time, who ordered the hit on Webster?" said the voice of John Dempsey. Both Grant and Bush sat forward in their chairs, waiting for the answer. They heard crying, then suddenly the answer came.

"Campbell ordered the hit, Peter Campbell," said Chalmers' voice. Grant looked at Collins with a smile on his face; he knew it was him and now he would have him.

"Sean, that's enough," said Palmer. As Palmer spoke, Collins turned the machine off.

"We've got him then, let's bring him in," said Bush, his voice sounded eager.

"Just hang on a minute, Mr. Vaughn is here for a reason," said Collins. He then looked at the man from MI-5, inviting him to continue.

"Gentlemen," said Vaughn, his accent was Mancunian, but posh. "I understand you have a ledger or a journal of some kind."

Grant held it up in front of him, and Vaughn took it and quickly browsed through it. Bush and Grant glanced at each other, neither of them knowing what was to come.

"I'll take this, gentlemen, if you don't mind," said Vaughn.

Grant was quick to reply. "But that's evidence," snapped the Kentish policemen, standing up.

Vaughn held his hand up to stop Grant. "What I am about to tell you must never go beyond these four walls," stated Vaughn.

Grant sat back in his chair and waited for what the man from MI-5 had to say.

"Peter Campbell will be taken care of. This investigation is now over, that comes from Number Ten," explained Vaughn.

Grant again was quick to jump in. "But the prime minister's involved."

"Like I said, Mr. Grant, this is the end of it," reiterated Vaughn. Grant looked at Collins, the DCI looked back with a shrug of his shoulders.

"So Campbell gets away with murder? What the hell is going on?" bellowed Grant.

"Campbell will be taken care of, our way. Without this journal and the recording, there is no evidence. This investigation is over, Mr. Grant. Do you understand?" said Vaughn, his voice slightly raised.

"Yeah, I understand," Grant said. He then walked out. If there was one thing that he didn't like, it was a cover up. The people not knowing, not being allowed to know, that really got up his nose. Bush acknowledged the three men in the room and chased after Grant. He caught him on the stairs.

"Come on Peter, you know the system, it's the way it has to be," said Bush.

"Then the system's a load of bollocks. You know it and I know it, so let's leave it there." Grant hurried down the stairs, leaving Bush where he was. As he walked through the main doors, Grant was still muttering to himself.

Chapter Twenty-seven

> It ain't over 'til it's over.
> --Lenny Kravitz

Peter Campbell had no clue as to what the prime minister wanted. He got a message through his office that the PM required the presence of the home secretary as soon as possible. Whatever he wanted, Campbell wasn't bothered because, in his mind, by next week he would be the main man in the news, the future prime minister of the United Kingdom.

He was met by his driver at six-thirty, outside the club in Westminster. The dark green Jaguar car sparkled under the street light, which had been coming into action over the last hour or so. For a winter's evening, it was still quite light and not very cold. Campbell was dressed in a suit with a thick overcoat. He wouldn't have noticed if it was cold or not.

Fifty yards or so down behind the green Jaguar a grey Vauxhall was parked. The driver was eating a piece of bread pudding which he had recently bought from a small bakers. Next to him on the passenger seat lay a small black box with an aerial protruding from it. He picked it up and thumbed the switch on the front. His eyes fixed on the green Jaguar, and he waited.

Campbell clambered into the back seat of the car and waited for his driver to get in. As he entered the driver's side, Campbell spoke.

"Not too quick, Paul. Let's keep the PM waiting a little longer, shall we."

"Yes, sir," replied the driver.

The driver started the engine and began to pull away. Suddenly the front of the car exploded, lifting the Jaguar fully six feet into the air. Campbell had no time to react. When the petrol tank exploded, he died instantly. Glass from surrounding buildings shattered as the car deteriorated, pieces of engine raining down on the street, people taking shelter in doorways.

The roar of the bomb seemed to go on for an eternity, but it was only a second at most. The Jaguar car was on fire in the middle of the street, many people approached it to see if they could be of assistance but the occupants had no chance.

Amidst the sound of screaming and burglar alarms, the grey Vauxhall crept down the street. It turned off just before the twisted wreck of the Jaguar, and the driver as he looked on, placed some more bread pudding in his mouth, and smiled as he drove away.

Peter Grant got home at around nine-thirty. Since leaving New Scotland Yard, he had spent the rest of the day in a dreary pub having a quiet afternoon with the company of a series of pint glasses.

Slightly drunk, he slumped into his favourite armchair. His wife lay asleep on the settee opposite, and he tried not to wake her. Next to him lay the remote control for the television; if he turned the volume down, he shouldn't wake Christine.

The policeman pressed the button on the handset, and the television sprang into life. Grant frowned when he realised the news was still on. Grant only caught the end of what the bespectacled man was saying. "...four other people were hurt in the explosion that killed the home secretary and his driver. Now over to Downing Street."

The picture changed to Downing Street, where the prime minister had just began to talk, his face slightly obscured by the mass of microphones in front of him.

"This callous act will not be tolerated by this government. The people responsible will be found and tried. Peter Campbell was a good man and a good friend, although he is no longer with us his work and plans shall continue."

The prime minister continued to talk, but Grant wasn't listening anymore. He put his head back into the chair and stared at the PM on the television.

"Hypocritical bastard," muttered Grant. Soon he was asleep.